Witch of the Black Circle

Maria DeVivo

Witch of the Black Circle

Maria DeVivo

4 Horsemen
Publications, Inc.

4 Horsemen
Publications, Inc.

4 Horsemen Publications, Inc.
1497 Main St. Suite 169
Dunedin, FL 34698
4horsemenpublications.com
info@4horsemenpublications.com

Cover by 4 Horsemen Publications, Inc.
Typesetting by Autumn Skye
Edited by Laura Mita

Library of Congress Control Number: 2021951177

Paperback ISBN-13: 978-1-64450-484-0
Hardcover ISBN-13: 978-1-64450-740-7
Audiobook ISBN-13: 978-1-64450-482-6
Ebook ISBN-13: 978-1-64450-483-3

Dedication:

For Babaysh – For "getting" me. No matter what I do or say. No matter how insane. You reel me in and let me fly at the same time, and that's a near impossible feat.

For Red – Thank you for babysitting those kids.

For Mo – It's always for you, and always will be for you … just maybe when you're much older.

Table of Contents

Chapter 1

Thursday, December 29th 1983
First Northport Assembly of God
Northport, Long Island, New York
Night of the Waning Crescent Moon

M*y mother believes I was cursed by a witch.* Not exactly an ideal way to introduce myself to a room full of strangers in a church, but it's not like I haven't said it before. It's not like I haven't tried to assert myself as the dominant, bad-ass, new chick or been the sweet and naïve little girl that no one would suspect of setting a fire in the girls' bathroom. This was a game of never-ending church meet-and-greets, and I learned how to play it long ago. It's all the same to me, really—this small new town with its idyllic gated communities and good, wholesome families that go to church at the appropriate times, drink lemonade on their sprawling front porches, and vacation out East to their expensive summer homes for two weeks in July. It's the scent of old money wafting in the air every time they suck their teeth at me in disdain and exhale with an uninterested, "That's nice, dear."

Been there, done that.

And I absolutely hate moving to a new neighborhood.

I've done this countless times my entire life. And now, as I sit in the circle of cold metal folding chairs among the members of this new youth group, I get to really contemplate *who* I am going to be to this group of soon-to-be-ex-strangers.

Might as well just be me. Not like I'm sticking around much longer.

The thought of being able to be *myself* for the first time in forever sends tingles up my spine to the base of my skull. I don't think I've ever *really* gotten to be *me*—the weirdo, the metal head, the angsty girl who loves Joan Jett and Lita Ford equally because I can! I like fire, death, and horror, and I say anarchy for the people because *why not?* These jocks and cheerleader types in this circle don't understand. They don't know me. The real me. They won't. And they can't. No one can.

I fold my arms across my chest as if to hug myself for such a marvelous revelation. Fuck it. I'm going full-blown "Joephie style" whether my mother likes it or not. Whether this dork of a youth minister who is spouting out some kinda crap about responsibility likes it or not. If my mother is forcing me to do this, to endure this *again* for the next six months, I'm going balls to the wall.

I run my exposed fingers from my cutout gloves up and down my forearms, scratching at the cotton material of my black Mötley Crüe t-shirt, kneading at the soft flesh of my thin arms underneath. *Six more months and I'm outta here.* The thought makes me giddy. Six more months and two major things are gonna happen—I'm turning 18 and I'm graduating high school. Then, I'll be free to leave the clutches of my mother's insane world of psychotic paranoia and fear. Sitting in the circle of soon-to-be-ex-strangers, I set the mental clock countdown, and smile to myself. It's decided—I'm going to be the tough, stand-offish Joephie. Grade A Bitch Deluxe. Fuck it. I've got nothing to lose.

I shift in my chair from boredom, bring my knees up uncomfortably to my chest, lock my arms tightly around them, and rest my chin on my knee tops. Strands of my razor-cut hair fall forward and down the sides of my arms, so I mindlessly pick at some of my split ends. The youth group leader stands in the center of the circle now, and his animated body language pulls me out of my distracted thoughts and daydreams. He continues to go on and on about something to do with teenage morals and duty to the church. He points his finger round the circle of the congregation and spreads his arms wide open in a rainbow arc as he preaches about the world, love, and the Lord.

I swear all youth ministers must have some sort of manual because this is the same wannabe sermon I'd heard from the last guy, with the same khaki pants and bright blue turtleneck shirt, and the one before that with the same horn-rimmed glasses and crew cut, and the one before that with the pretty wife and even prettier mistress.

"Make good choices, blah, blah, blah."

"Have God in your heart, blah, blah, blah."

"Obey the teachings of your parents, blah, blah, blah."

Nothing has changed except the person speaking and the level of reverberation of their voice off the church's stone walls. I knew the First Northport Assembly of God would be no different than the center in Brooklyn, or Far Rockaway, or Lynbrook, or Hicksville, or Massapequa, or Deer Park... same, same, same. Same types of people, same schools, same non-denominational youth group trying to promote peace and harmony to the same bunch of disinterested kids who said "amen" then went off to get stoned in the park. Only this time, the ending is going to be different. This time, I won't be packing up my belongings in a frenzy during the middle of the night. This time, I'm gonna walk out the front door of my mother's house, two fingers in the air in a peace sign, and never look back.

My thoughts must have gotten away from me, and I only realized I was smiling hard to myself—open-mouth, teeth bared, the whole nine—when I notice two other kids in the group huddled together, glancing my way and whispering to each other from the corners of their mouths. I let my face fall suddenly into a purposeful scowl, and they quickly turn their gazes to the floor. I snicker on the inside. They're wearing their coats. It's not *that* cold... but then I look around at the other kids here, and they're all wearing their coats too, just me and the minister aren't. Weird. Whatever.

4

"And so, my friends," the leader dude booms, "I leave you with this: keep your good thoughts flowing and your actions to match."

My face twists at the leader's awkward closing sentence. I can't help it! But it's apparent it's his thing to say because the group tops it off with thunderous applause. When I realize this, I give a little half-hearted clap too. To say I'm unimpressed is an understatement. I've seen better performances.

The congregation gets up from their chairs and scatters around the room—the chatter from their individual clusters creates a surge of sound of incoherent conversations. Alone, I saunter over to the refreshment table and stare hard at the cups pre-filled with powder-mix fruit punch and opened boxes of chocolate chip cookies. This is like amateur night. Nothing like the pizza parties in Lynbrook.

"Hey," a high-pitched female voice says from behind me.

I swivel my head around and am met with the girl and boy who had been whispering about me earlier. "Hey," I say back and stare them both down.

"I'm Kit," the girl says pointing to her chest nervously, "and this is Dan." She thumbs her finger to the boy next to her.

"Hey," Dan says, half-heartedly lifting up his hand in a limp wave.

"Joephie," I say flatly because a part of me wants to scare them away. *Leave me alone. I don't need any friends. I just need to ride out these last six months and...*

"You new in town?" Dan mumbles, and Kit nudges his arm.

"What gave it away?" I reply sarcastically, and they both give an awkward chuckle, which breaks some of the tension I've previously created. I have to admit, I kinda chuckle too.

"Will you be starting school after winter break?" Kit asks.

I pause and take a moment to observe the pair. I can't figure out their deal. Her body language says that she's more into the guy than he's into her, but that could just be my own over-dramatic mind creating something that isn't there. I've always been skeptical of new people, even when my mother constantly tells me to keep an open mind, broaden my horizons, and branch out to people I wouldn't normally connect with. Kit's a cute girl with a soft-blonde bob and meticulously swooped bangs to match, but she wears a double-breasted, pink trench coat that's buttoned up to her neck. I know right away she's not my people. She's not gonna get me. "Yeah. Northport Prep."

"Neat! That's where I go!" Kit exclaims and claps her hands.

I jut my chin out in Dan's direction, and my black hair falls down to my mid-back. "You?"

"Northport High." He unzips his denim jacket revealing a Mötley Crüe t-shirt underneath. With the same chin-jut motion, he grunts, "Got the new album?"

"Shout at the Devil, man," I say, and I lift my right hand and give him the devil horn sign.

Dan raises his left forearm to return the standard metal-head greeting and reveals circles drawn up the length of his arm in black ink. Scribbles of circles with elaborate flames wildly curving upward or what looks to be thorns protruding from the bottoms—like someone plotting out the design and placement of a tattoo. Everyone does it as like a boredom thing, but his look... I don't know, *deliberate.*

I think Kit sees me staring at his ink-filled arm because she quickly grabs it and lowers it down to his side. "Really, Dan?" she gushes with an exasperated sigh that is too fake to be believed. "I guess you haven't listened to that new band I told you about. Slayer? Far superior and heavier than Mötley Crüe."

"Yeah, yeah," he says dismissively.

Now my interest is piqued. How the hell does this Barbie doll know about Slayer or have an opinion on the band for that matter? Guess I pegged that one wrong. "You listen to Slayer?" I ask.

A pink blush blooms on Kit's pale cheeks and her shoulders slouch forward a little. It was a demure little motion, but I caught on real fast. *It's part of her act. They're weirdos like me.*

"Slayer's good," I say, and she smiles knowingly at me.

Dan opens his mouth to start to say something, but he's interrupted by the approaching youth group leader.

The leader's toothy smile shows his immaculately white teeth that light up like little lanterns against his unnaturally tanned face. In his hand, he carries pamphlets with the name and logo of the church. "Welcome!" he says to me in a jovial voice, a typical happy-go-lucky-preacher voice that makes my skin crawl. In the center of the circle, he was unassuming, an ordinary preppy dweeb of a man. But up close, there's kinda something. A vibe. An aura.

I quickly take a step back to create some distance between me and him, but I brighten my face up and say a cheerful, "Hello!" so as not to be so conspicuous.

"It's always great to see new blood!" he booms as he extends his hand to me. "I'm Trent."

I receive his hand to shake it, but something in the handclasp sends a wave of ice up my arm. Trent must have sensed something as well because his eyes narrow down at me, trying to pinpoint or evaluate what had caused the strange energy that passed between us. "Joephie," I manage.

He quickly releases our hold. "Ahh, as in the Archangel Jophiel." He breathes in and closes his eyes. "Divine beauty of God."

Kit and Dan chuckle again, and I give them a questioning look, like *What is up with this dork?* "Nooooo…" I start to say slowly, my voice lilting up to a high note, "as in Josephine."

The three of us can hardly contain our giggles, and Trent opens his dark eyes with a condescending glare. "So, I see you've met Katherine and Daniel, Miss Josephine." Kit and Dan give each other a side-eye glance, like two little kids being scolded by a parent.

I pick up on the exchange and widen my eyes at them for a second. "Yep."

"And what brings you to our ministry? Are you new in town?"

"Uh, yeah. We moved around the block a few days ago. As soon as the Christmas break is over, I'll be going to Northport Prep."

"Where did you move to?" Kit asks.

"Over on Harbor Hollow Road."

She brings her hands up to her mouth in an excited way and squeals, "I'm literally around the block from you! We could walk here together!"

I'm taken off guard by this creature before me. Her voice, dress, and mannerisms all scream that she's some teeny-bopper Valley Girl, but there's a layer beneath the cliché façade that interests me. Is she a straight-up poser, or is she a demon in disguise? I guess only time will tell. *If I haven't scared her away yet...*

Trent purses his lower lip and nods his head. "Well, you don't need to be scared or nervous. We're like a big happy family here."

"It's cool beans. I'm used to it. I move around a lot."

"Ahh... military brat?"

"Nah. My mom is single right now and moves around for work. So new town, new crowd, new school, new youth group. My mom thinks this is a good way to meet people and get in with the 'it-crowd.'"

Of course, that was the excuse for our constant moves. With my biological father long dead, there was always a new boyfriend, new husband, new job, and new opportunities, but all that was a complete lie. I know the truth—my mother was running and hiding, making it so that I didn't have any connections or long-term ties or friends, making it so that I wasn't influenced by druggies, gangs, or covens.

Trent hands me a pamphlet but doesn't immediately release his end of the grip. He narrows his eyes again, as if trying to scan me, to figure me out. "Such a dutiful daughter you must be to follow the wishes of your mother. She's scared for you, isn't she? She hates how you dress. Hates the music you listen to. Tells you it's just a phase. You'll grow out of it. Right?"

There's an uncomfortable vibe that passes between us, and he's staring at me so hard that I feel compelled to look away. Finally, he notices my discomfort-level 10 and lets go of the pamphlet. "Something like that," I say to his shoes.

"Well, Josephine, the only friend your mother hopes you make is Jesus Christ. And I assure you, He's here now. You just have to open your heart to him."

"C'mon, man!" Dan interjects. "It's her first night here! Ease up on the God-stuff so early on! Really, Joephie, the group isn't like, uber-religious like that."

"Now, now, Daniel. We *are* in a church, and…"

"Trent!" Kit exclaims.

"Look," Trent continues, "all I'm saying is we are in turbulent times. I hear the music you listen

10

to, and I see the devil symbols and your black clothing. I know what it's like to have teenage angst, and I know you use this iconography as an outlet of expression. For many, it's harmless. For some, it's sinister. We are here to guide you between the two. The devil is everywhere, guys. We need to be on guard."

"So we can save our souls, right?" Kit asks with a sarcastic tone.

"Exactly, Katherine. Exactly."

"Well, we're not Satanists, I promise you that," Dan says, but there's a hint of a joke in his statement, and Kit taps her foot on his, as if to silence him.

Trent smiles and nods his head. "I know, I know. Shout at the devil, right? I'm actually more worried about you guys getting STDs than summoning Satan. Look through the pamphlet. That's next week's meeting—'The Beauty of Abstinence.'"

The three of us laugh as he walks away.

I pick up a plastic cup of fruit punch and take a swig. "What's his damage?" I say, motioning in Trent's direction.

"Oh, don't mind him. He means well," Kit says in a hushed tone.

"Yeah, he had a rough childhood and shit and is just trying to give back to the community. He's like a reformed Manson cult member or something crazy like that," Dan continues. "That's why he's got that holier than thou vibe."

"More like a creep-o vibe," I say.

"Nah, he's a harmless goober," Kit concludes nonchalantly, but I'm not 100 percent convinced. Something about Trent doesn't sit right with me. He has an aura, a presence, a... a... *something* that I can't pinpoint. I continue to stare at him from across the open vestibule of the church—sizing him up, watching his movements and gestures. It's as if he's gliding from group to group with his beaming smile and light-up teeth, shaking hands and passing out pamphlets, absolving sins, and doling out advice. Swift, almost unnatural motions. And if I try real hard, I can almost zone in on his voice and his voice alone. Tune everyone else out and isolate his audio above the others.

"Keep your good thoughts flowing!"

"Good job!"

"Go in peace!"

And every phrase sounds hollow and empty because they aren't real words to my ears, just noise. *Does that mean he's not a real person?* I stare and stare, and right before Dan interrupts my trance, I notice again how Trent was the only one besides me who wasn't wearing a jacket.

Does that mean I'm not a real person too?

Stop with the crazy thoughts, Joephie. We're not doing this right now...

"So really, why did you move here?" Dan asks.

I blink rapidly, as if awakening from a spell, and shake my head side to side to regain my focus. "The same reason I move anywhere. My mother believes I was cursed by a witch."

Chapter 2

Wednesday, January 18th 1984
The Turner Residence
165 Harbor Hollow Road
Northport, Long Island, New York
Night of the Full Moon

K it sits across from me at the kitchen table, and I'm trying so hard not to look at the scratches in the fake wood-looking Formica tabletop. It's so scratched up—so deep in some spots—that the dirt stains don't ever seem to be erased no matter how hard they've been scrubbed. I often tell my mother to bite the bullet, get rid of her 1960s crap furniture, and update our whole house, but she refuses to splurge. Says she has more important things to spend her money on— like the higher than usual rental payments on these new digs, or my up-and-coming career as a college student. *Wherever that may end up being.* "Besides, if it ain't broke, don't fix it," my mother sings, so we'll just continue to live in covered up, repurposed shit.

Odd. That seems to be symbolic of my entire life.

Kit blabbers on about some stupid calculus formula, and I let her think she's helping me with something I don't know. I don't have the heart to tell her that I'm totally beyond calculus and that I learned all this at my last school, so I space out while she continues to enthusiastically ramble. One thing I noticed about Northport Prep is that for a private school, they're a little behind in the curriculum department. It doesn't matter either way to me though, because if that's the case, I'll be able to skate by for the next six months. Really, the only two things holding up the integrity of that institution are the preppy-to-the-max uniforms and the veil of strict rules and regulations.

Kit's blue eyes grow huge at some mathematical revelation, and I give her a soft smile. This display is mildly amusing—she's doing some "real-world" good, and I get to tra-la-la in my head. She's fun to watch. When she raises her eyebrows, the tips of her poofy bangs touch the edges of her perfectly curled eyelashes. It must tickle to feel the strands of hair dance lightly and so close to her eyes. When she talks, her heart-shaped mouth makes these perfect shapes and her lips glint against the pendant-lighting above the table. I bet she wears flavored lip gloss—the kind that comes in those little rectangle tins. She slides the cover over, swipes her finger over the top of the product, and spreads it all over her lips.

I bet it's strawberry. No, maybe cherry. Nah, I bet she's a bubblegum kind of girl.

I could ask, but I'm too entranced with the thought of it to open my mouth. She and I must look like quite the duo sauntering down the hallways at school—the blonde haired, blue-eyed Beauty Queen Angel arm in arm with her sidekick Goth Girl. Her pink, glossy lips say, "Hi everyone!" My black, inky lips scowl, "Fuck off!" And ya know, I would have thought that my black hair and makeup would have been like a homing beacon for the other freak-o kids at school, but I guess aligning with Kit put a stop to that. *Because they only know what they see. Because they don't know who she really is.* They don't know there's a darkness that brews in the chamber of her heart. I don't think even *she* knows how deep it runs. But I can sense it. I feel it. I *know...*

Regardless, she's adorable as she fervently taps her finger on the page of the worn-down textbook like she's showing me the X mark on a treasure map. Maybe she thinks she's a pirate? Eureka! We got it! And there's *cosx* stitched onto her eyepatch. I'm waiting for her to say "Arrrrgh" or something piratey.

"Joephie? Are you with me?" she finally says.

I must have spaced out a little too hard. "Yeah, yeah," I say as I snap back to reality.

"You know, you need to like, know this stuff," she sings sarcastically. "For the SAT."

"Yeah, I know. I'm good." It must be obvious that I'm not interested. "I don't really need the help. You know this is really for..."

"You *are* gonna take the SAT, right?" she asks, cutting me off.

"Yeah, yeah. Of course," I say, trying to avoid the topic.

The timer on the stove dings and my mother waltzes into the kitchen. "Of course Joephie is taking the SATs!" she chimes in, and I try hard not to acknowledge her. I look down at my short, ragged fingernails and pick at the black nail polish. Flakes of paint flicker off and get stuck in the cracks in the table.

"Hi, Mrs. Turner," Kit says sweetly.

Mom puts on a mitt, takes out a tray of chocolate chip cookies from the oven, and places it on the counter. "Hello, Kit! And please, call me Nancy!"

I raise my head to indulge in the delightful smell of fresh baked goodness wafting in the air.

Kit blushes. "Yes, ma'am," she says in her reserved voice.

My mother smiles back, and just as she's about to say something corny, the doorbell rings, and she rushes through the hallway to answer it. Kit and I look at each other and say "Dan," at the same time.

Sure enough, it's Dan at the door. "Hello, Mrs. Turner."

"Call me Nancy. Let me take your coat." Blah, blah, blah.

When Dan comes in, he throws his backpack onto one of the empty green swivel chairs and plops himself next to me in the other one. I'm relieved that all four chairs at the table are now occupied so as to not give my mother any bright ideas about sitting and chatting with us. She had followed Dan into the kitchen to put the warm cookies onto a serving dish. *Shoot me.*

He puffs out his chest. "Check it out!" he declares as he shows off his black t-shirt with the white writing.

Kit and I both shake our heads.

"You made that?" Kit asks, unimpressed.

"What did you use, white paint?" I interject.

"Yeah, dude. Why? Not like you can buy them or anything yet."

"Yet," I say. "You coulda just waited or something."

"Nah. It's a one-of-a-kind! A Dan Barone Original!"

My mother turns around, cookie dish in hand, and looks at him. "What is it?"

Dan stands up proudly and moves his shoulders side to side showing off his masterpiece—white letters sloppily painted across the chest and an upside-down pentacle underneath the word.

The plate in her hand trembles slightly, its movement reflecting the tiny earthquakes firing off in her core. "Slayer? What's Slayer?"

"Only the newest, most intense heavy metal band from out of Cali," he declares.

Mom tenses up as if all the muscles in her body clench at once. Her eyes go wide, and her grip tightens on the cookie dish. It's a subtle gesture, but I recognize it all the same. She's done this before, had this conversation before. Lived this

17

fear before. Clearly, she's uncomfortable. Clearly, she's bothered by the handmade t-shirt with the demonic symbol on the front. She opens her mouth to say something, but I give her a look that screams, "Don't you dare!" Her breath hitches in her throat and she pauses, rethinks her words, and says, "Oh you kids, and your crazy music," in that fake, I-don't-mean-a-word-I'm-saying mom voice.

Kit and Dan don't seem to hear it, but I do.

But mom can't help herself. I see her distress written all over her face. Her weary, tired eyes are surrounded by deep-set crow's feet that bear the remnants of old, black eyeliner caked in the creases. "Black clothes. Black hair and makeup. Darkness and depression. Why all of that? What does it all mean?"

"Mother!" I scold.

She places the cookie plate in the center of the table, and both Dan and Kit instinctively reach for one. "No, really Josephine," Mom continues. "I just don't get it! We parents do everything we can to support you guys, love you guys, raise you guys right. This is your rebellion, right? Like how we had in the 60s. Peace, love, hippie-style. Right?"

I stand up and move to usher her out of the kitchen. "Sure, Mom. Whatever. Whatever you say."

"Look at sweet Kit here. Why can't you dress like her, Joephie? Would it kill you to put on a cardigan or a turtleneck? Maybe something pink or baby blue? You look so nice in blue. It brings out your eyes."

It's apparent that Dan and Kit are holding back their laughter out of respect. Dan shoves his cookie all the way in his mouth so as to keep himself from bursting out. My face twists. "Are you serious, Ma? Don't let the Barbie doll, Valley Girl act fool you! Kit was the one who introduced Dan to Slayer! She's as much of a freak as I am!"

"It's just that," she continues, "children your age are so susceptible to the power of persuasion..."

Smiles wash over Kit and Dan's faces, and they lean in like little children waiting to hear some fantastical story.

Through gritted teeth, I mumble, "I knew this was a bad idea," but the others ignore me. I know they heard me, though.

"... and drugs, and the devil. Parents are just trying their best to raise good and decent children, but with so much sin and temptation and..."

"Well, and because Joephie was cursed by a witch, right?" Dan blurts, interrupting my mother.

Mother freezes in her tracks and glares at me. Our eyes lock, and I scream at her on the inside—scream at her for being so paranoid, delusional, and toxic. She reaches into her pocket and pulls out her pack of Marlboro cigarettes. "Oh?" she questions. "Is *that* what she told you?"

I quickly jump up from the table and grab her arm before she can light up. For a split second, I see myself grabbing her head and smashing her skull against the porcelain sink, and out of the corner of my eye, my hands are bloodied with her brain matter. But I shake my head swiftly because I know it's just my imagination. "Just go inside, please?" I whine as I guide her to the hallway.

"Wait!" she protests. "Aren't you going to introduce them to your grandma?"

"Enough!" I yell. "Just go!" With a final little nudge, she disappears into the depths of the living room and when I return to the kitchen, Kit and Dan are as silent as mice.

"What?" I demand. "I told you guys my mother is nuts!"

"It's okay, Joeph," Kit says. "All of our parents are totally weird."

"Or like Trent says, 'it's just a phase,'" I say as I reach for a cookie. I can't deny that my mother's homemade chocolate chip cookies are the best, but that doesn't mean I can't have an unnatural disgust for her. "You guys have no idea what she's like or the things she does."

"What do you mean?" Dan asks. "She's a killer baker! How bad can she be?"

I suck in the question for a second and contemplate how much about my mother or my past I actually want to dive into right now. *How bad can she be? Oh, dear Dan, you have no idea! Should I tell you the one where she dragged me up the steps of a Catholic church by my hair and dunked my head in the holy water font because she had a dream that told her my soul was in danger?* I was five, but I remember it clear as day because that was the first time she'd decided we couldn't stay in one place for very long. *Or what about the time when she spoke in tongues during my third-grade talent show, and the vice principal had to escort her out into the parking lot while I was singing my horrid rendition of Dolly Parton's Jolene?* I could go on and on about the embarrassments and injustices inflicted upon me by my life-giver, but I merely respond, "Forget it."

"Well, if she's so bad, why do you go to youth group like she tells you to?" Dan says, popping another cookie in his mouth.

I cringe on the inside. "Because it was the one thing I promised her I would do. It was that or send me off to some kind of boarding school. So I figured it was the easier thing to do. Why the hell do *you* guys go?" I bark, annoyed.

"Well, Kit and I have been going since we were kids, but as we got older, the guidance counselors at school told us that we could use it for volunteer hours on college applications 'cause it was like a religious thingy or something, and all we had to do is put down that we were a youth peer counselor or some shit like that." He pauses and thinks for a second. "Hey, Joeph. You never said you lived with your grandmother."

I roll my eyes and exhale. "Well, if you consider ashes in an urn on the mantle 'living with someone' then you can go say hi to Grandma Jane in the den."

Dan stares at me wide-eyed, and Kit makes a little gasping noise in her throat.

"Starting to make sense now?" I ask, my voice rising in inflection at the end of the sentence.

Kit picks up her pencil and nervously taps it against the textbook. "Do you guys wanna get back to business?"

Dan reaches over to his bag and pulls out his math book. In the front pouch, I notice a small novel with a black cover. "Hey," I say, nodding my head in the backpack's direction. "Whatcha reading?"

"Uh, nothing," he answers, shrugging his shoulders.

I put out my arms and tap my fingers together like a baby grasping at something. "Lemme see it!"

"Nah. It's really nothing," he repeats, but he's unconvincing, and it makes my curiosity burn a hole in my brain.

Kit's curiosity is piqued as well, so she stands up and moves behind the chair with the back-pack. "Now, now," she sings. "No secrets here, Dan!" She grabs the bag from the chair and pulls out the book. "*The Satanic Bible*?"

Dan quickly shoots up from the chair, snatches the book away from her, and cradles it to his chest as if to hide the cover from us. "Shhhh…" he admonishes as he looks side to side, assessing if my mother was in the vicinity or not.

I hold out my hand again. "What are you reading *that* for?" I ask. "Give it here."

Reluctantly, he turns the book over to me, and I examine the cover, the spine, and the back like an investigator studying a piece of crime-scene evidence. Only I don't have on rubber gloves. I've known about this book. Heard about it. Knew the story of the author, Dr. Anton LaVey and his Church of Satan. Practically every youth ministry I had attended had mentioned the evil of this piece of literature at some point in time: *If you even look at the book you can be possessed. Being in its presence alone can have a profound effect on your heavenly soul. Dare not open or read the pages for fear of infiltration by a powerful demonic force.* But as I actually *hold* the book for the first time in my life, I feel … nothing. No fear. No wonder. No spooky taboo. I press the book in my palms trying to feel for any 'other-worldly' vibrations or indication that if I open it up, I will be damned to hell. But no. Nothing. Zip. Zilch. And more lies and deception from my past teachers come into clear view. "Dude. It's just a book."

"Yeah, I know it's just a book," he huffs, grabs it from me and shoves it back into his bag.

The three of us sit back down in silence for a few minutes.

"You okay, man?" Kit asks, concerned.

"Yeah. Fine."

Clearly, he's not.

"Where'd you get it?" I ask.

"*Why'd* you get it?" Kit emphasizes.

Dan looks behind him and scans the kitchen again. Then, he moves his upper body slightly across the table as if to beckon me and Kit to huddle in. We oblige him, and he speaks in a soft, hushed tone: "Thomas. This guy from my school. He's got the connection with that Ricky kid and the Knights of the Black Circle."

"The Knights of the Black Circle?" I ask. "What's that?"

Dan glares at me and holds up his arm revealing the faded black circles drawn up and down his arm, over, and over, and over. I had thought they were just silly drawings borne out of boredom, but...

"They wanted him to read the book and know some stuff before they accepted him," he continues. "Thomas said he could probably get me in, too and told me what passages to study and shit."

Kit's pretty eyes widen and her bangs touch her eyelashes again. "He knows the Acid King?"

A sneer forms on Dan's lips and he nods. "Uh huh."

"Wait," I protest. "What are you talking about? Who are the Knights of the Black Circle? What's an Acid King?"

"The Knights..." Dan explains, "they're a group. Local. They do stuff. They know stuff."

"Magic stuff," Kit says, lowering her voice like she's revealing a heavily guarded secret.

"You mean, they worship the devil? Like a cult?" I ask in semi-disbelief.

"You can say that," Dan says. "And this guy Ricky..."

"The Acid King?"

"Yeah, the Acid King. He's like, hardcore, man. Super into this shit. They do, like, animal sacrifices in the Aztakea Woods."

"So, why do they call him the Acid King?"

"Drugs. He's really into drugs," Kit says.

"So, you're saying this druggie, Devil Lord communes with demonic spirits in the woods with his group of disciples? Sounds kinda lame-o to me."

Dan exhales loudly in the huddle, like he's unsure of my reaction. Like he's doubting whether he should have told me about this. "Well, like I said, they *know* stuff."

"This is something you guys want to be a part of?" I ask directly to Kit.

She closes her eyes and nods.

Dan runs his fingers through his shaggy, black hair. His light-brown roots are coming in, and I wonder if he gets Kit to dye it for him. "I don't know, man," he says, breaking my thought. "I've heard a lot of stories, and I just kinda want to know, ya know?"

I know. Like I've said to myself a thousand times since I got to Northport—I know. I've done this all before, met these types of people before—kids who thought they were badasses, smoked pot between classes, listened to Led Zeppelin backward, and swore to God they heard voices. I didn't hear shit, and I knew they were liars. "I don't know," I say hesitantly. Because I'm not quite sure how I feel about jumping into this kind of stuff with these people. I've only known Dan and Kit for like a month and…

"Told ya we shouldn't have brought it up," he says to Kit.

"Dan! It's fine. Joephie's cool."

I look back and forth at the both of them, like: *Hello! You do realize I'm sitting right here, right?*

"Please tell me you're cool, Jo," she pleads with me, her eyes forlorn and desperate.

I squint my eyes and my face screws up as if to say, *Are you kidding me?*

"They all *think* we're into this shit," Dan says, making his case. "Why not actually give it a shot?"

I shrug my shoulders. "Whatever, man. Just how do you know this Acid dude is on the level?"

Dan props his elbows up on the table and cuffs the sides of his face with his hands, forcing Kit and me to squinch in closer to him so we can hear whatever secret it is he's got to tell. "Oh, he's the real deal, alright. A few months back, Ricky went out to some cemetery with dead soldiers and shit and was digging up dead bodies. He took a hand and a skull and was gonna use them in some advanced ritual or something."

"No way!" Kit squeals. "I call bullshit on that!"

"I'm telling you, guys. Thomas even showed me the hand."

A pulsing wave washes over the area above my eyes and rocks me with blinding pain. I sit back in my chair and lean my head back, hoping it will pass. Behind my closed eyes, I envision the hand that Thomas kid showed Dan—decrepit and rotting, a gold wedding band sliding off the ring finger, violently yanked from the rest of the arm at the wrist. The image is so real and so vivid, it's almost as if Dan is waving that hand around in my face right now, but I know he's not.

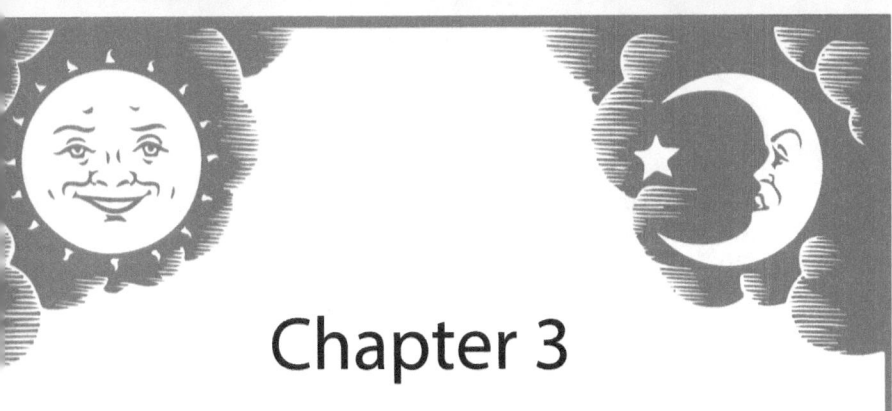

Chapter 3

Thursday, March 8th 1984
First Northport Assembly of God
Northport, Long Island, New York
Night of the Waxing Crescent Moon

R ain steadily pelts the wooden roof of the
rundown church. It's a calming sound—
one of rhythm and consistency. I have to admit, I
do prefer the kind of rain that's violent and angry
and accompanied by bright explosive flashes and
deep growls from the sky, but for now, the sounds
of the constant tapping against the rooftop and
the misty wind thrashing against the stained-
glass windows are soothing enough to put me in
a trance-like state.

Kit and I walked over to the meeting tonight
before the rain started. She met me at the corner of
Pickett and Sutton, and we cut through the sump
to save us a total of a minute and a half walk-
time. The sump is nothing more than a sunken-in
section of land. It was probably formed from a
sinkhole, or series of sinkholes, and the natural

erosion of rainwater and the elements carved out a valley-esque piece of land in the corner of the neighborhood park. Over time, people built tunnels through there for storm water runoff. Guess the water has to go somewhere. Regardless, this place eventually became a hangout for the lovers, stoners, and weirdos.

The second we reached the church steps, the sky started to cry, so I guess it was worth it. We were the last ones to show up, and Trent had given us an aggravated glare when we walked in, so I deliberately dragged my chair across the linoleum floor. The metal made a scraping sound that had forced him to stop his opening speech until I had gotten myself settled. He didn't appreciate that too much, and I didn't care. He really gives me the creeps sometimes.

Dan and Thomas were already there when we arrived. I think Kit is a little jealous because she obviously is head-over-heels in love with Dan, but he's kinda more interested in what's going on inside the Knights of the Black Circle rather than what's underneath Kit's clothes.

And like all of the youth group meetings I've attended at the First Northport Assembly of God, I vaguely pay attention to the man in the center of the group, and instead, I focus on the sound of the rain.

"You can find the devil just about anywhere you look," Trent says loudly. I suspect he knows I'm not really listening to him. "Satan is a force that is ever prevalent in our world—it is greed, power, sin. We can see the devil in money, politics, and music." He exits the circle of chairs, goes to the far corner of the room, and drags over a cart on wheels. It's one of those black metal double-deckers like they have at school. When the teacher brings out the A/V cart with the TV on top, everyone cheers because we know it's movie nap time! But Trent's cart has a record player on top and a stack of records set next to it.

"Through the power of music," he says as he drags a long extension cord to the outlet on the wall, "the devil can speak to us and try to manipulate us. It all came to light in 1969 when there was some controversy over the Beatles song 'Revolution 9.' Fans declared that there was a hidden message saying that Paul McCartney was dead, and it just blew up. Was it true? Some people claim they heard it. Others say they just heard gibberish. But there are instances, from The Beatles to Frank Zappa, where messages can be heard in a string of songs—messages that are *deliberately* inserted to tap into our subconscious minds and convert us to the dark side."

I shift in my chair, rest my elbows on my knees, and cradle my cheeks in my hands. He's mildly gotten my attention now because I've played this game before, and I wonder if he knows something that I don't. *C'mon Trent, play that funky music, white boy.*

"It's called backward masking, and it's a very serious legal issue. The state of Arkansas passed a bill last year requiring that records with backward messages have a warning label on them."

"But isn't this just subjective?" one of the guys in the group says. I don't know him except for here in the youth group. I think his name is Seth, or Serge, or Simon, or Something. "Isn't it just mish-mosh and like, what people think they hear? Mass hysteria. Like, if I tell you to listen to a song backward for a message and then ask you to tell me what you hear, you won't be able to decipher anything but babble, but if I tell you to listen to a song backward and I tell you it says 'Satan rules,' your brain will automatically scan the audio until it hears 'Satan rules' in the static."

"Well, Seth," Trent responds.

Ah-ha! I was right! I smile out loud at my awesome memory skills, but Seth must think I'm smiling at him. He looks at me and smiles back (even though I'm *not* smiling at him), and his grey eyes kinda do this twinkly thing. They look like shadows flickering in the woods at night. They're so interesting to look at, like I want to see more. I bite my lower lip and continue to smile, and this time I *am* smiling at him.

"You do make an excellent point. It's called pareidolia—a delusion of the senses that can be influenced through the power of suggestion," Trent booms again, breaking Seth and my stupid, quasi-flirty smiling-fest.

"So isn't it all just pare… whatever you called it?" Thomas says.

"Yes, and no. Some is and some isn't. Some of what we hear in these messages are definitely a fabrication of our collective mindset, some of what we hear are deliberate messages purposefully inserted by nefarious people trying to spread the word of the Anti-Christ, and some of it is... well... something else."

Kit raises her hand as if she was in class or something.

Trent acknowledges her with a head nod.

"If these musicians can insert these bad messages in their music, couldn't they also do the opposite, and like, put in good messages?"

"Oh definitely! But why would they? The good ones don't need to hide their intentions. They say it loud and say it proud. It's the sinister ones who need to be sneaky about it. They're the ones who need to embed their messages of hate, sin, and corruption. When it's done on the subliminal level, you don't even know it's happening. You don't even know the effect it's having on your mind and your soul."

He pauses for dramatic effect, and a hushed murmur rumbles in the congregation. If he didn't have the attention of fifteen teenagers before, he does now. *Including mine.*

"Take, for instance, your clothing. A lot of you wear these heavy metal band t-shirts. But look at the shirt that Daniel wears."

Dan nervously looks around the room as all heads turn in his direction.

"Stand up. Show everyone your creation."

Dan rises from his chair with a shit-eating smile on his face. He puffs out his chest to proudly display his black, homemade Slayer t-shirt with the white letters and upside-down pentacle.

Trent stands next to him. "Daniel, I've seen you wear clothing like this before. And I think maybe one of the reasons why you do it is partly to show off your personal style and beliefs, and maybe another part is to get a rise out of me."

Giggles pop up from the circle. Dan opens his mouth to protest, but Trent raises a silencing hand. "It's okay. It's okay. I'm not offended. I applaud you for staying true to your beliefs, whatever they may be at this juncture in your life. When I was about your age, the people I knew, even me… we did things that when I look back on them now seem so stupid, petty, and dangerous, all because we believed in something…" Trent sighs heavily and it echoes above the sound of the wind howling outside, "… in *someone* that we really shouldn't have believed in. I'm just trying to help you guys not make similar mistakes. I take it that Slayer is a music band you listen to?"

Dan nods his head.

"And they're what? Heavy metal? Is that what you classify them as?"

Dan nods again.

"Why the name Slayer, though?"

Dan's eyes narrow. "Huh?"

"Slayer? Why did they choose that name?"

"Probably because it sounds dark, cool, and evil," Seth contributes.

Trent puts a hand on Dan's shoulder and gently pushes him back into his chair. "Maybe," he says slowly as he walks back to the center of the circle to where the record player is. "Maybe it stands for something else, though. Like, a subliminal message hidden in the letters. Maybe Slayer is an acronym for something even more evil. Like, Satan Loves All Your Endless Rambles, or Satan Laughs As You Eternally Rot."

I tire of Trent's "the-devil-is-everywhere" sermon, so I raise my arms high above my head and crack my back.

"Josephine? Do you have something you'd like to add?"

I freeze mid-crack, surprised. He must have thought that I was raising my hand like Kit had done before. Like a good, little, obedient child of God would. But I *do* have something to say, something to contribute. "You said before there was *something else*." I make the motion of air quotes as I say the last part of the sentence.

Trent looks puzzled. "Excuse me?"

"You said about the backward messages. They can be perceived, or implanted, or something else. What did you mean by that?"

The wind outside pounds harder against the church, making the windows rattle in their casements. Trent stares me down, like he's angry with me for bringing up what he said earlier, or angry at himself for mentioning it in the first place, or a little bit of both. I can't really tell. His face darkens in a way that is both scary and fascinating, and I try to decode whatever message he is hurtling in my direction. The room grows quiet and still, and he and I hold each other's gazes for a few awkward seconds. His eyes scan me, and my head starts to hurt. It feels as if his stare is trying to pierce and probe the insides of my brain. Quickly, I look away from him when the pain travels to the back of my eyes. I think I see him smirk.

Finally, he reaches for a record on the wheelie cart and holds it up for the group to see. Against a black background is the band's name written in a brownish-red font that's supposed to give the appearance of dripping blood. It's a simple design, but definitely one that is strong enough to convey an eerie statement. "Blodheksa," he begins. "They're a Norwegian heavy metal band and are pretty popular in the underground metal scene in Norway. Their name means 'bloodwitch' in English and judging by the name and the cover of the album, I don't think I need to explain too much about what they represent."

Everyone gives a nod of agreement, but I just fold my arms across my chest.

"This is their debut album that came out in 1976. Since their debut, they've released an album each year. I'm going to play you one of their songs, and you'll see it's very rudimentary—poor equipment, poor recording, the vocalist isn't the best, the skills of the musicians aren't the greatest."

"So how do they sell albums if they suck so much?" someone interrupts.

"Well, that's debatable. Is there something more going on here? I don't know. Let's listen and talk about it."

Trent takes the record out of the case and places it on the player. Once the music starts, there's a collective cringe among us. He wasn't lying; it's awful. Ear-splittingly awful. It sounds as if it were recorded in someone's cement basement on the very first 4-track machine ever invented. All I know is this: they would never be able to hang with the bands here in the States! The drum track overpowers the guitar, and the vocals are muffled and barely audible. Not to mention it's in Norwegian. They could have been singing about playing checkers for all we knew, but Trent doesn't let the song play in its entirety: it's *that* bad!

"Thank God!" someone shouts out when Trent pulls the needle off the record, and we all laugh.

"I know, right?" he agrees. "I mean, I don't particularly like the music you guys listen to either..." and he glares hard at Dan for a second, "but this? It's pure garbage."

"Flaming pile of garbage!" Seth shouts.

"That track is titled 'Inn I Det Svarte' which translates to 'Into the Black.' I'm not going to translate the words for you, but knowing the title of the song and the name of the band can probably give you an inkling of what's going on. You see what I was saying about the guttural feel to it, though? It wasn't professionally recorded, so any backward masking would have been nearly impossible to do. Now, I'm going to play the song in reverse for you, and I want you to just keep an open mind and listen."

"But the forward words aren't in English," Dan says.

Trent ignores him and starts the record player up. Gingerly, he moves the record against the natural flow of the platter, confusing the poor needle to speak in opposite of what it's normally accustomed to. The crowd waits patiently—waiting to hear something, anything, other than the backward, garbled gibberish of the untalented band.

I close my eyes, half paying attention and half tuning in. I don't really expect much to come from this. To be honest, the rain tapping on the rooftop sounds much better than the crap coming from the turntable. I sway my head to both of the independent sources of sound, and my brain kinda starts to mesh the two together, syncopating them, melding them, swirling them to create a new sound, a new rhythm, with new instruments and a new voice. It starts out at a low frequency, like a wave of a rumble, and suddenly crescendos to a crash of thunder where there was none before. I feel it in my stomach. Like cracking me open from the inside out. Splitting wide an energy and a force that had been dormant for forever. Dormant to awake. Day to night. Beneath the rumble is a voice. Not the vocalist for Blodheksa. Not my subconscious. But a voice—dark and gravelly that punches through the haze, rain, thunder, energy, and reverse music. A voice speaks words to me in an ancient tongue that I can't decipher in my brain, but I can translate in my soul. It awakens me. Cracks me open like an egg. Implants in me a third eye. Gives me sight. I see for the first time in my life. A newborn babe. I sway and sway. I get lost in the words. *I get lost in the woods.* Consumed by the voice. Swept away by the storm outside and in.

In an instant, it stops. My eyes open wide, and I see Trent has pulled the arm off the record. The only sound left is the remnants of the rain. But there's something that has been awakened inside me, like a surge of electricity. Like a newfound sense of purpose and power. I feel... *alive?*

"So," he begins, "did anybody..." His voice trails as he scans the congregation. Bewildered faces stare back at him, and he gives a little nod. A knowing nod. No one offers up any thoughts or conversation starters. Could it be I wasn't alone in that experience? What in the hell *was* that, anyway? "Alright," he says clapping his hands together with finality, "I will see you guys next week. Keep your good thoughts flowing and your actions to match!"

Unnerved by his quick dismissal of us, the congregation gives a weak, obligatory applause and everyone rises to leave. There's no after-refreshments tonight, no cliquey groups huddling in their usual spots, just a get-up-and-go vibe.

My head throbs. Not like a migraine, above-the-eye-pain, but a throbbing sensation pulsating in all the soft spots in my brain. It radiates red. I don't know how I know that—I just do. I feel red. I don't know how I know that either. Something happened to me in there, and I feel off—just not right. I think I need to just go home and get some sleep.

Dan and Thomas meet Kit and me by the front door, and I'm fully prepared to call it a night and walk myself home. "Hey," Dan says, "whatcha guys doing now?"

"Nothing," I reply. "I guess just go home. I'm super tired, and I have a headache from the stupid music."

Kit eyes me sharply. There's an urgency in her expression, and I know that was definitely not the answer she was wanting to hear from me. "Whatchoo guys doing?" she answers coolly, nonchalantly.

Thomas smiles widely, and a cut on his upper lip splits open, filling my nostrils with the scent of his metallic blood. "Wanna see it?" he sneers at me.

I huff in disgust. "If that's some kind of sexual invitation, I think I'll pass," and I nudge Kit's reluctant elbow over the threshold.

"Nonono...." Dan stops us. "Ya know..." he dips his head and covers the top of his mouth, "the *hand*."

Kit grabs my hand and wrings it up and down. "Are you serious?" she beams.

"I know where it is," Thomas says. "I can take you guys out there if you want."

"Is that kid Seth gonna come, too?" The words come out of my mouth before I realize what I'm saying.

"Nah," Thomas replies. "He had to talk to Trent about something after the meeting."

"Alright, let's go!" Kit says. She grips my hand tighter as if to say, *Please, Joephie, please!* I just want to go home and rest, but Kit is like a little kid in a candy store, and she's so cute with her lips all pursed out, pleading with me to come along. And I have to admit, my interest is piqued at the thought of seeing some dead guy's decrepit old skeleton hand.

I rub the side of my head, and we walk down the church steps. "Just don't put the radio on too loud," I say as I get into the back seat with Kit.

Aztakea Woods Parking Lot
Northport, Long Island, New York

Thomas turns off his headlights as he pulls into the far-right side of the parking lot—away from the glow of the streetlamp, hidden in shadows of the misty night. A group of four teenagers gather around what looks like a dark blue Trans Am—I don't know, it could be black, although it's hard to tell in the darkness. They look over at Thomas's car with defensive stares when he shuts the engine off, but when they realize we're not a threat, they continue on with their business as if we aren't even there.

Thomas grips the steering wheel nervously. "He's over there in that group," he says with a little shake to his voice.

I play dumb and ask, "Who's over there?" But I know exactly who he's talking about.

"Ricky!" he shouts, and he continues to stare straight ahead. "I gotta go get permission before I can take you there," and there's a faraway, glazed-over look in his eyes.

"Are you high?" I demand.

Thomas shakes his head as if snapping out of a dream. "What? No, no. I'm not high…" he pauses and looks at Dan with a smirk, "…yet!"

Dan laughs and goes in for the high five with Thomas.

Kit and I look at each other and roll our eyes. "I thought you said you knew where the hand is though," Kit says. "Why can't you just take us out there? Why do you need permission from the almighty Acid King?" She winks at me, and now it's our turn to laugh.

Thomas swivels his head to us in the back seat. "Because you just don't do stuff like that when it comes to Ricky. You just don't." There's an intense darkness in Thomas's eyes and a serious expression on his face that I didn't think possible from his usual teenage jokey manner.

Thomas is scared of Ricky, I conclude in my head.

"Dude!" Dan calls out. "They're gonna leave!"

"Oh shit!" Thomas yells. He opens his door, jumps out, and races across the lot to the Trans Am.

"He dropped out of school, ya know," Kit says as the three of us watch Thomas rush up to the group.

"Who? Thomas?"

"No, Ricky," Dan says. "They say he got kicked out of his house. They say he lives in these woods. They say he trips out and talks to spirits and shit."

"Oh," I answer calmly. "They say a lot of things, don't they? Any of it true?"

My mother says I was cursed by a witch.

"Who knows?" Kit says. "But it's a pretty well-known fact that Ricky is not the kind of guy you mess around with."

Raindrops pelt the roof of the car, and we sit in silence for a few moments before Dan asks the question we probably all had swirling in our minds: "Did you guys actually hear anything from that Blodheksa song being played backward?"

Kit's thigh muscle twinges in an uncontrollable spasm. I feel a sudden motion of the vinyl rub up against my own. "Did you?" Kit asks quietly.

"Nah," Dan says in a faraway voice, but I know he's thinking about something, figuring out something, *remembering* something. His reflection from the side window shows me his pensive brown eyes, and the raindrops that slide on the glass make it look like he's crying. Because yes, he's crying on the inside. Crying because his brain, heart, and soul won't allow him to understand the voice he heard. "You, Joephie?"

I pause for a second, contemplating if I should or shouldn't tell them what I experienced. *I mean, how can I put into words the surge of energy that cracked open in my body?* I breathe and make my attempt. "I can tell you th…" I start to say, but suddenly Dan shushes me, and we all get quiet and pay attention to the scene at the Trans Am. It's probably best I don't tell.

The voices from the group grow louder, and I think I hear Thomas say, "Why not?"

"You heard what Ricky said, man!" a boy shouts. "Not now!"

Thomas puts his hands up defensively. "Alright, alright. Forget it," he relents and turns around to walk back to us. The other boys get into their car and peel out of the lot; the worn-down wheels screech and skid against the pavement like crazed lunatics escaping from an asylum.

When he gets back into the car, he pounds his hands on the steering wheel. "Shit! Fuck!"

"So…" Dan says, "I'm guessing that's a no?"

"Yeah, Dan. It's a 'no.' Ricky doesn't want to have any new people involved right now. He thinks there are people following him and shit. It's not a good time."

I grip the back of Dan's seat and scoot my body up and in between the gap of the front passenger cab. "But you know where it is?" I plead. "Just take us out there! Like, we're already here! How in the hell would he ever know?"

"No way, man," Thomas says, fear rising in his shaky voice. "He'd know. Trust me, he'd know."

Chapter 4

Friday, April 6th 1984
Seth's House
95 Whispering Woods Drive
Northport, Long Island, New York
Night of the Waxing Crescent Moon

*W*hen the cat's away, the mice shall play. Or so the saying goes or something like that. Thomas and Dan pick up me and Kit at the corner of Pickett and Sutton—it's our usual meeting spot because it's halfway from my house, close to the sump where the guys like to go smoke dope, and halfway to the First Northport Assembly of God. It's alright with me to meet there because it keeps my friends far away from my mother and the insanity that is my household. I stop myself for a second, realizing that I referred to them as my friends. Are they? Am I even capable of having friends? Or being a friend? Because at the end of the day, I'm kinda a shitty friend, to be honest. While Kit's all talking about graduation, summer vacation, and planning some trip out to the

Hamptons for the four of us, all I can think about is getting the hell out of here. I have zero interest in sleeping on the beach or exploring some cozy seaside town or collecting rocks to make a night-time bonfire. Zero. Zip. Nada.

'Cause I'm a shitty friend. And people who are shitty friends don't give a shit about the excitement and interests of those around them.

I just need to get far, far away.

Speaking of the Hamptons, turns out that Seth from the youth group is like, ultra-loaded. His parents have a summer house out there, and this weekend they went out to open it up in preparation for spring break at the end of this month. Instead of going with them to help, Seth decided to stay home. And Seth decided to throw a party...

Okay, okay... I'll admit it—there *is* a part of me that's a *little* excited. This is my first senior party this year, so that alone is kinda cool, I guess. Kinda gives me an excuse to wear my black mini-skirt, new Mercyful Fate t-shirt, and my black Dr. Martens boots. And this is also the first time I'll be hanging out with Seth outside of youth group, which is kinda cool, I guess. Dan and Thomas said that there are going to be guys from the Knights of the Black Circle there, so that also mildly piqued my interest. For whatever reason, Thomas thinks Ricky, The Acid King, will be there too. After that night in the parking lot and the way Thomas and Dan go on and on about him, I'm very curious to meet him.

In the back seat of Thomas's car, Kit rests her head on my shoulder, and I snake my left arm up to gently pet her hair. It's soft and silky in the back, but the teased top brushes up against my cheek like broom bristles. The distinct smell of Aqua Net hairspray wafts in my nose. "You use a whole can tonight, Kitty Kat?" I joke.

"Har har," she retorts, and she scooches closer to me, laying her hand dangerously high on my upper thigh. "Listen," she whispers into my ear. Goosebumps blossom on my forearm. "I think Thomas is gonna try to make his move tonight."

"Huh?" I say, confused. "On me?"

She digs her French manicured nails into the exposed flesh of my leg, and another round of chills shoots through my body. "Shut. Up," she scolds forcefully through gritted teeth, but the music is so loud in the car, I don't think the boys could hear us if they wanted to. "Like you didn't know? Like you didn't wear this cute little miniskirt for no reason?"

"Him? *That* Thomas? *Our* Thomas?" I say, motioning my head toward the front seat. The guys are completely oblivious up in the front.

She nods, and a few strands of her stiff hair go up my nose.

"Stop. That's totally insane. I'm not..."

Suddenly, Thomas swerves the car violently into Seth's driveway. The boys laugh uncontrollably as Kit sticks out her tongue and points to the inside of her throat in the 'gag me' motion. I can't help but smile. She's too cute.

"So," Dan says before we ring the bell, "Seth is already in with the Knights. I think this is kinda like an audition for us. Like, tonight's the night."

"Word on the street is Ricky is gonna be there, so like, he's kinda tight with them and all, so..." Thomas says.

"You sure you wanna do this?" Kit says to me.

"I'm observing," I say. "Out of curiosity." Because I am. And I'm not. "Really, Kit. I don't feel like..."

Thomas nervously runs his hand through his hair and rings the bell. Remnants of black drawn circles run up and down his arms, and I kind of shudder. *Like, dude, you can't even wash yourself properly to get that all out?* "You all read the book, right?" he says, referencing *The Satanic Bible* and whatever rule the Knights have about being well-informed on the topic.

Kit and Dan fervently say "yes," and I nod.
But I didn't.

Seth greets us at the door with a big "Hello" and leads us into his palatial home. Inside, the party isn't as big and wild as I had originally thought it was going to be. I had expected beer cans littering the hallway and people passed out on couches and loud music blasting throughout — maybe, a puker in the bathroom, or a little group smoking some pot out of a bong on the back patio. But no. No such scene is to be found. Just another guy and girl sitting around the kitchen table, drinking beers, and talking. *I'm so overdressed for this*, I think to myself.

"Hey guys!" Seth calls over to the group. "These are the chicks I told you about from Prep. Kit and Joephie."

Eyes scan us over awkwardly and a collective "hey" rises from the bunch. They go to Northport High with Seth, Thomas, and Dan, so Kit and I are odd ladies out here tonight. Kit grabs my hand and squeezes, and we both nod our heads back at them.

"Susan," she says.

"Bill," he says.

The doorbell rings again. "Help yourself to anything you like," Seth says as he goes to answer it. Thomas heads straight for the beer in the fridge, and me, Kit, and Dan make our way to the circular kitchen table and sit down. I sit in the closest chair next to the huge bay window, and for a moment, I stare out into the vast darkness. Seth's yard is backed up to the tree line of the woods, and I glimpse the shadowy trees dancing gently in the nighttime breeze. They're like multi-armed gods beckoning me to join them, and I think I'd rather be out there with them, my kin, than inside here with strangers. The trees glow and sway, and in my chest, I feel a thump—not my heartbeat, but a second heartbeat, like an extra thud that keeps my heart pumping extra and everything and nothing at all. I breathe in deep, and Kit kicks my foot from under the table, and I snap back to reality and meet her eyes.

"You okay? You with me?" she asks with her super sweet, super concerned childlike voice that reminded me of a baby doll from some episode of *The Twilight Zone*.

I rub my left temple. "Yeah, yeah. I'm good." I force a little smile.

A Ouija board is at the center of the table, and at each corner of the board is an unlit candle, but the planchette is missing. And I get the overwhelming suspicion that this isn't your average weekend senior party.

Thomas pulls out two beers. "I bet that's Ricky at the door," he says as he cracks the top of a Bud and tosses the other to Dan.

"Nah, man," that guy, Bill, says. "It's Carmen."

Thomas's eyes go wide in disbelief. "Seth never told me Carmen was coming!"

I raise my suspicious eyebrows. Now, I'm not particularly attracted to Thomas or anything, but Kit said he was gonna maybe ask me out tonight, and like, this Carmen chick situation seems to have gotten him rattled and everything. It's not like I'm jealous or anything, but it's so totally obvious that Thomas is shaking in *his* Docs over a girl … who isn't me.

"Besides," Susan says, "Ricky got locked up!"

"Locked up? What happened now?" Thomas wails.

"Cops got him on the whole grave robbing thing," Bill fills in. "He should be out soon though. I'm guessing his parents are gonna bust him out of there or something."

"He didn't get arrested, Billy!" Susan chimes. "They just hauled him in for questioning about some drug thing in Amityville."

"Whatever, Suze. He ain't coming, so…" Bill concludes, and I look over to Thomas and watch his face fall with disappointment.

Seth walks in with Carmen. She's an average-looking girl with shaggy-brown hair and heavy black eye makeup. She looks like every other non-descript metal-chick, stoner girl, and I can understand why Thomas would have been attracted to her. It's obvious they have some kind of history because Thomas puts his head down and shuffles over to the table to sit down next to Kit. I honestly don't care about their history because I have three more months until all these people become a part of *my* history.

Carmen dangles the missing planchette in the air between her thumb and forefinger, and the group cheers. Seth turns the lights out and announces, "Alright! Let the séance begin!"

Séance? This should be fun…

Carmen places the planchette in the center of the Ouija board and lights the four candles at the table. I nervously jump when the plastic indicator plops down. "This isn't like in the Exorcist, ya know," she says to me with a biting tone. Kit kicks me again under the table as if to silence me. I grit my teeth to myself and hold my tongue.

"We're good with eight?" Seth asks her.

She sits down. "Yeah. Eight's fine. It represents the cardinal and intercardinal points of the compass."

"Listen, guys," Seth says. "If this works, trust me, I will reward you! My grandfather always told me stories about how this house was built on top of some kind of burial ground and all that mumbo-jumbo. If it's true, we can dig up the yard and get whatever it is we need to open the portal. Ricky got the hand and the skull, but they said it didn't work. I think we need more. So we're gonna try to get more."

"That sounds boss!" Thomas exclaims.

"No need to go grave robbing when your house sits on top of some dead Indians. Possession is nine tenths of the law, right?" Dan adds.

No Dan, possession is when you mess around with other-worldly entities and have your body overtaken by a demonic force, but who's worried about that?

Carmen claps her hands. "So, I'm guessing everyone knows the rules on this. Put your forefinger lightly on the indicator, no pushing or moving. Seth asks the questions because it's his house and he's the one initiating contact, but your energy is going to help to usher in the spirit. Like, think of it like this: the spirit needs a conduit, a bridge, in order to connect to this world. Our collective energy is going to be that bridge. Sometimes it will help to envision a color surrounding you. Just relax, take deep breaths…"

"And keep your good thoughts flowing…" Seth blurts out, and he, Thomas, and Dan go into a fit of giggles.

I have to admit, it's kinda funny because what Carmen was saying did kinda have that "Trent-closing-act-vibe."

She's not amused. She glares at Seth hard from her North position, and the candle directly in front of her throws dark shadows across her face, giving her a totally angry look. And then it hits me—she believes in all *this*, and she's offended that her fellow member of the Black Circle isn't taking it as seriously as he should. Like, Seth's offense is severe enough to kick him out. He straightens up his back when he realizes she is none-too-pleased, and he settles himself down. "Try not to talk," Carmen says calmly. "Actually, don't talk at all." She pauses and places her finger on the planchette. "Okay, let's start."

Everyone shifts closer to the board and follows Carmen's lead. I barely touch the indicator, like my finger kinda hovers there fighting for space among the other fingers. Kit can hardly get close enough to be involved and a wave of panic comes over her face, so with my finger, I twist it around hers and guide it closer to mine. She gives a little sigh of relief, and her body eases up. Poor thing. Her palpable panic kinda broke my heart for her a little.

"We call to you, Oh Great Beyond," Carmen declares in a strong voice that exhibits control and command. "We seek your other-worldly power and knowledge. The Knights of the Black Circle ask you to bless us with your presence."

Wait? Us? As in, all of us? Does this mean we're in? Are we now a part of the Knights?

Seth tilts his head up and scans the room. "Is there a spirit present with us?" he says to no one in particular.

Immediately, all eyes shift to the planchette for a response. Bill kicks Susan underneath the table for some reason, and Kit makes a cute squeaky sound in her throat. But nothing happens.

"The Knights of the Black Circle invite you to join us and bless us with your presence. You are welcome here in our domain," Seth proclaims.

They've done this before. They've memorized some kind of script.

Again, they look at the planchette, and again, nothing happens. Seth eyes Carmen from his South position, and worry darkens his eyes. She's not yet convinced that contact won't be made because she nods to him, urging him to continue.

"M… maybe we need to…" Susan whispers, but Carmen quickly shushes her, and Susan's mouth closes with a quick gulping sound.

"Are we in the presence of a spirit?" Seth asks again. The indicator moves a centimeter to the right and Kit tenses up again, but it's not enough to prove that it's working.

"Everyone just needs to relax," Carmen advises, but the doubt in her voice is evident.

Okay. Fine. Let's play.

I breathe in, close my eyes for a moment, and think back to the night in the church at youth group and to how I *felt* when I heard that song being played backward. Human words can't describe that feeling, but I try to remember and revisit every tingling sensation. My whole life I've always felt some kind of *connection*, some kind of *something*. Whether it be dreams, weird coincidences, or déjà vu shit. I've always kinda felt like I'm walking neither here nor there, like I'm trapped between the spaces of reality and some foggy world. Christ, that doesn't make any sense whatsoever! I don't know, maybe because my crazy mother always told me I was cursed that I naturally put that label and feeling on myself, or maybe she was telling the truth...

Even with my eyes closed, I see the shadows from the candlelight dancing in the room, and I subconsciously try to push all my energy through my body and out of my fingertips. *Be the conduit*, Carmen had said, and I'm not 100% sure what that's supposed to mean, but I try to envision a white light radiating from my body and forming an arch from my finger on the planchette to the Ouija board. I've never played this game before, and I don't believe it has any more significance than just being a silly parlor game, but I guess as a newly indoctrinated member of the Circle, I might as well give it a try.

A push-and-pull feeling starts in my stomach and works its way into my upper chest, and suddenly I'm weightless, like my whole body floats above the table and chair. I open my eyes and look down, and see that, no, in fact, I am *not* levitating. But it feels like I am. Like I'm just an inch above the surface of the chair, as my once steady finger twitches uncontrollably over the indicator.

"Is there a great and powerful entity present?" Seth asks again.

Of course there is, a voice says to me in my head.

Suddenly, the planchette begins to slide across the board to the upper left corner of "yes." The air in the room grows thick as everyone holds their breath. Carmen raises her eyebrows and a smirk sweeps over her face.

"D... d... did you guys do that ... 'cause I..." Susan stutters. Bill kicks her again, and she freezes.

"Spirit!" Seth gushes. "We welcome you and thank you for joining us. We call upon you to aid us in our search. Are you from our time?"

Nope, the voice answers in my head, and the planchette glides to the upper right corner "no."

"Are you from the last fifty years?"

No, the voice says, and the planchette slides down and back over the "no."

Seth shifts in his chair and smiles. "Are you from the last one hundred years?"

Negative, the voice tells me, and the indicator rotates over the "no."

"The last 200?" There's a quivering urgency in Seth's tone, like he's starting to get scared that we summoned something that won't help him.

Nope.

The planchette does its little sway-dance over the "no" again.

"Do you know why we called upon you, spirit?"

Yes, because of those goddamn bones, the voice laughs to me.

When there's no immediate response from the board, Seth repeats, "Spirit! Do you know why we called upon you?"

I close my eyes and envision the word "BONES," and sure enough the planchette begins to move.

"B… O… N… E… S," Carmen reads each one out loud in surprise.

Seth whispers a triumphant "yes" to himself. "Thank you, oh great spirit! Yes. We are looking for the bones buried on this property. Can you tell us where they are? Where are the bones?"

There's no response from the voice I had previously heard. I don't know where the bones are buried. No one here knows where the bones are buried. And the voice sure as hell doesn't know where the bones are buried…

And I freeze.

'Cause now that I think about it, the voice that had been speaking to me was all too familiar. The voice was sarcastic, unattached, and rude.

And then I realize—there was no actual voice because the voice has been *me* the whole time. *I* moved the planchette. My fingers surge with heat as I try to come up with a response for the board. I'm blinded by a searing pain that jabs me above my left eyebrow. I close my eyes and wince from the ache, and as I do so, an image flashes behind my eyes: *Seth in the woods in the back yard, tied to a tree, blood-soaked clothes, crying out for his mother.*

Soon the planchette begins to move again over the letters, and Carmen spells it out slowly. "S… E… T… H… S… D… E… A… T… H." And after the last H, the indicator swings violently down to the "goodbye" slot. Everyone quickly removes their hands from the plastic and jumps back into their seats.

"Seth's death?" Bill repeats. "What the fuck was *that*!?"

"It could mean anything," Carmen says calmly, but it's obvious she's containing her fear. "Sometimes the messages from the other side aren't communicated properly."

Seth's eyes go wide. He's visibly upset.

"I don't think it counts anyway," Thomas says. "Joephie didn't have her finger on the indicator."

"What?" I bark.

"I was watching you. You lifted your finger and rubbed your head. Then the thingy moved to say Seth's death. So it doesn't count."

"Yeah," Dan adds. "Maybe, like, the spirit got pissed that you broke the bridge or whatever, so it said something bad about Seth."

Carmen glares hard at me. "It's possible," she says.

"Or maybe there wasn't a spirit at all," Kit says trying to ease the fear in the group. "Maybe it was just Thomas and Dan screwing around!"

The group laughs a little, and Susan blows out the candles. Everyone gets up and starts milling about the kitchen, except me. I stay put at the table and observe.

"I'm going to the bathroom for a sec," Kit says, and I give her an *okay* nod.

Bill and Susan go into the sunken den off of the kitchen to watch TV. Thomas and Dan gather around the open fridge pulling out trays of food and beer while Seth and Carmen stand by the patio doors, gazing into the woods out back. I keep my eyes on the Ouija board at the table and pretend to not listen to their conversation.

"We'll try again in a few days," he says to her.

"Okay," she relents. "I'd just really like to have the offering for Walpurgisnacht."

"Look, if it's gonna happen, it's gonna happen."

"I can't go digging up some Colonial War grave, Seth. My father would flip out if I got arrested for something like that! I'd lose my scholarship and…"

"Don't worry, Car. We won't let it come to that. We'll get them. One way or another, we'll get them."

"But Ricky said…"

At the mention of Ricky's name, Thomas practically leaps over the kitchen island to get to them. "What did Ricky say?" he asks. He sounds like such a doofus butting in on their convo.

"Nothing, Tommy," she says in a low voice.

Tommy? I've never heard anyone call him Tommy.

"Look, if Ricky needs help with something, just ask. I'm all in. Dan too. Whatever it is, we got it!"

"Thanks, bro," Seth says as he claps Thomas on the shoulder. "I appreciate that. I'll let you know," and he turns around and goes into the den with Bill and Susan, leaving Carmen and Thomas standing alone.

"Can we talk?" he asks her after a moment of awkward silence.

"Tommy, I don't know, I just…" her voice trails.

He slides open the patio door. "Five minutes. Just give me five minutes."

Her foot taps on the tile floor, and she puts her hands on her hips in an annoyed stance. When she realizes Thomas isn't saying anything or going anywhere, she huffs, "Five minutes. That's *it*!" And the two disappear into the back yard.

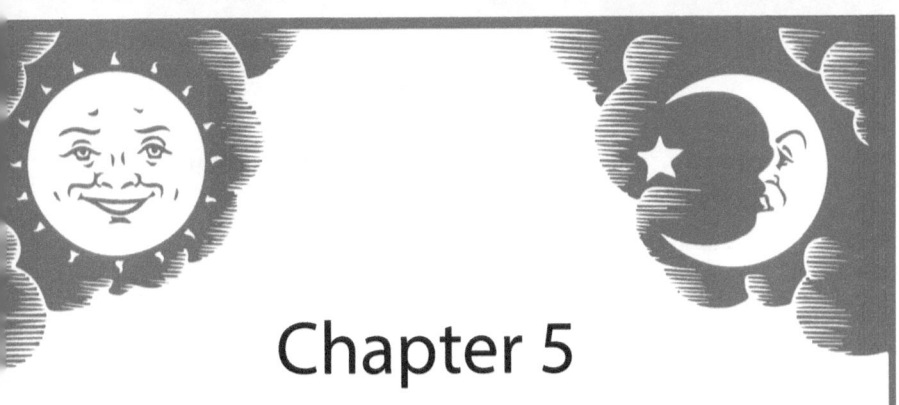

Chapter 5

Monday, April 30th 1984
Walpurgis Night
The Turner Residence
165 Harbor Hollow Road
Northport, Long Island, New York
Night of the New Moon

My eyes are closed, and I'm resting on my bed with Black Sabbath's "War Pigs" blaring into the circular foam coverings on my Walkman's headset, but anyone standing within a few feet of me would still be able to hear the grinding guitar riff and Ozzy's strong voice bellowing about Satan's wings and probably grimace and turn their nose up at me. So many times I've heard my mother say, "You're going to blow your eardrums out!" or "Don't you have a headache from all that noise?" or "Why do you listen to that filth?" or "What did he just say?" But I don't care. Whatever. And I know Black Sabbath came out with a new album last year, but I'm definitely fonder of the older stuff. "Paranoid" is my favorite. Besides, I'm pumping myself up for tonight—Walpurgis Night.

Witch's Night.

The night when witches contact and commune with the devil.

Dan has been a little secretive on what the plan is for tonight, but I'm okay with that. I'm quite sure it involves dead body parts and chanting and candles. I'm still very curious if this group I've now aligned myself with has any kind of real power. The more I'm around them, the more the answer becomes "no." But since the backward messages and the Ouija board incidents, I feel different. Like there's something there that I can't put my finger on. Like, I know stuff. I feel stuff.

Anyway, after the party, Seth and his buddies tried to summon the spirit a few more times to locate the buried bones on Seth's property. I wanted so badly to tell them that there wasn't any spirit there in the first place, that it was just me playing with them. Kit and I weren't invited back because Carmen said we were "outsiders who probably disturbed the natural flow of things anyway." But I knew the real reason was because Carmen wanted to keep Thomas as far away from me as she could. So instead of eight, they séanced with six, and not to my surprise, they came up empty-handed. Of course, Kit was upset because she was prevented from seeing Dan and because this meant she and I weren't really *in* the Knights of the Black Circle. Unlike Kit, I don't have this intense desire to belong to a group like that. Besides, I don't think they can do the things I know I can.

I usually wait for Kit at the corner of Pickett and Sutton, but lately she's been picking me up at my house, and the two of us kinda go alone. We still hang out with Dan and Thomas on a regular basis, but apparently the night of Seth's party, Thomas really only did need five minutes when he had sex with Carmen in the woods, and they decided to get back together after that. Just as I had expected, Carmen and Thomas had been an item from way back in junior high, and they were the on/off couple all these years. I'm guessing she's the only girl he'd ever slept with, and maybe he was the only guy she'd ever slept with too, so going back into their routine maybe just felt natural for them.

It just kinda made things with the four of us weird. I mean, I don't like Thomas like that, but as a group of five, it worked as a good balance. But Carmen got thrown into the mix, and six feels weird. Plus, I'm not really keen on other girls who aren't keen on me. Typical girlhood jealousy—she found out that Thomas was into me and felt the need to posture, so the four of us don't really ride together much anymore.

"Your friend is blowing her horn like a crazy woman, Josephine!"

I open my eyes to my mother perched over me, staring down with her big green eyes like giant googly golf balls. Her hands are on her hips, and she's scowling. I wish she could see how utterly ridiculous she looks right now. "Okay," I answer curtly.

"If you didn't have that turned up so loud, you would have been able to hear it!"

"Okay," I repeat and rise from the bed.

"You know, Josephine, your friends *can* come inside. I don't know why you have to keep them at arm's length."

I huff loudly. "You're kidding me, right?"

She stares at me with a blank expression, as if the last seventeen years of constant moving around was normal or even just something that happened inside my head. "What do you mean?"

"Really, Ma? I don't have time to get into a discussion about why I choose to distance my friend-life from my home-life 'cause that's pretty long list."

She shifts her weight from one hip to the other. Her high-waisted jeans make a swishing sound that grates on my nerves. "Where are you going anyway? It's a school night!"

"Youth group meeting," I lie because I can't tell her the truth. I can't tell her that tonight is Walpurgis Night and that the Knights of the Black Circle are planning a ceremony to open a portal to a hell dimension and that some kid they call The Acid King is planning on calling forth Satan himself to do his bidding. Because that would just sound ludicrous. And that piece of information would cause a fight, and she would try to stop me from going or have me thrown into a mental institution again or something.

Mom's face screws up. "I thought youth group was on Thursdays?"

"Yeah, well, something came up, and Trent needed to switch the day." I brush past her out of my bedroom door and make my way outside.

I skip outside and into the back seat of Kit's car. She smiles brightly at me, and I return the gesture. Her soft blonde hair is pulled back into a ponytail, and her freshly cut bangs fall evenly and perfectly right about her brows. Dan is in the front, and he throws up the devil horns sign to me, so I return the gesture.

"Thomas is going with Seth," she says as I slam the door and sit in the center seat so I can prop myself between them. "Carmen and Thomas had a fight or something. I think they're like, broken up for this week or something."

"Nothing new," Dan mumbles.

"Wait!" I interrupt, unconcerned with Thomas and Carmen's love life. "Going *where*?"

Dan laughs slyly. "Oh, it's about a half-hour drive to Amityville."

"What's in Amityville?"

"Only the most haunted house in the entire world! The Amityville Horror House? Ron DeFeo? Butch? Ten years ago, he killed his entire family and…"

"Yeah, yeah, yeah," I say waving my hand dismissively. "I know the story. The Lutzes. The haunting. The book. The movie. All very compelling stuff, but why are we going there?"

"It's Walpurgis Night, Joeph!" he says to me like I'm some kind of simpleton.

"And don't forget the night of the new moon!" Kit adds.

"Yes!" he exclaims. "That too!"

"So... they're going to do the ceremony at that house?" I probe.

"Yep!" Dan sings.

"Seth said that Ricky said that the Horror House is the perfect spot to open the gateway to hell. He's bringing the hand and the skull," Kit adds.

"Seth said that Ricky said that the only other place that would be better to do this would be on the grounds of that old, burnt-down town in Massachusetts..." Dan chimes.

Kit huffs out a little sigh. "Well, we ain't there, so..."

"Even though we couldn't dig up anything else from Seth's house..."

"Wait!" I say, interrupting Dan. "Don't people like, live there and shit?"

"Oh, yeah, yeah. It's fine. The front yard usually has a lot of people around. Tourists and shit. We're gonna meet everyone on the side yard. Everyone else will be distracted, so they won't even know what's happening."

"Who's *everyone*?" I ask.

"Ricky and his crew, and me, Thomas, and Seth."

"What about me and Kit?"

Dan runs his hand through his stringy hair. "I don't know, man. Seth is okay with you guys, but

I'm not sure how the Knights, like, deal with girls. Like, I think the Knights are a guy's only thing. Girls are just the arm-assistants."

"Fuck you!" Kit squeals and jerks the car onto the highway ramp.

"I'm sorry! I'm sorry!" he apologizes. "I have no control over these things. It's like a fraternity, ya know? Besides, Seth still has to vouch for me and Thomas, and he *just* got in tight with them. I'm in no position to be making demands or even suggestions. Can we just wait and see how this plays out?"

"So, what? Are we supposed to stay in the car or something?" I challenge.

"Yeah," he says in a low, embarrassed tone. "Something."

The original excitement of the night is now deflated. I sit back in my seat, away from the two of them as Kit drives the rest of the way to Amityville in silence.

South Ireland Place and Ocean Avenue
Amityville, Long Island, New York

We arrive around 8:30 p.m. and park the car at the corner of South Ireland Place, directly in front of the Amityville Horror House on Ocean Avenue. Unlike what everyone had assumed, there isn't anyone around. Guess Walpurgis Night is just another Monday to these normal people in town?

I don't know what I was thinking, but I could see this place getting lots of traffic come Halloween, the American traditional spooky holiday. But Walpurgis Night? Please. Only freaks like us know what that means. Only freaks like us would even consider celebrating this ancient feast day.

The street is not very well lit, so it's hard to tell if there's anyone out there. Which, of course, is the perfect opportunity for this all to go down—a secret ceremony on someone's front lawn, opening the portal to hell under the cover of darkness. Sounds all malicious and scary. It's kinda laughable, to be honest.

"Seth's car is right over there," Dan says, pointing to a car to the right of us. "I'm gonna go see what's what. You two stay here. I'll come get you if we need you." Dan opens the passenger side door slowly and skulks out and down the street. I take the opportunity to hoist my body over the back seat and up front next to Kit.

"Fuck him. Now, he can ride in the back on the way home!"

Kit giggles. The sound is sweet in the echo of the car, but there's not really an echo—that's my brain trying to capture the sound and record it to memory. It's like a jingly bell on a snowy morning—the sound reverberates off mammoth roof icicles, or is that a church on Christmas morning? I don't know what I'm thinking right now.

Kit exhales. "Well, this sucks."

"It blows."

"Blows chunks."

"Blows super chunks!"

She giggles again, and again I try to capture that sound. I want to remember it forever...

"Ya know, I'm starting to think this whole Knights of the Black Circle is a bunch of bullshit," I say. "I mean, I just don't get how they operate, or what are the rules, or who's in command, or how does this all work! This Ricky kid? What's his deal, man? Why is everyone so afraid of him? Why does everyone kind of tiptoe around even conversations about the dude?"

Kit leans her head back on the car seat and fishes for a cigarette in her sparkly pink purse next to her. She pulls out two, lights them both up, and passes one to me. There's an impression of her pink lip-gloss on my filter, and it tastes like watermelon when I inhale. "Ricky's a legend, Joephie. You know, he's not even from Northport! But everyone knows who he is, and everyone knows what he does. The Knights? They're just a group. You know how it goes. They're secondary to Ricky though. People don't call him The Acid King for nothing ya know."

I take a long drag on my cigarette and exhale loudly. "I don't know. Kinda not buying it. Like, on the one hand, I understand they want to be all culty, but then you get people like Bill and Susan who are *clearly* only in this for the weed. So which way is it?"

Kit rolls her window down a crack and exhales from the side of her mouth into the smoky night.

"It's both, I guess. You can't deny that séance at Seth's wasn't fucked up though."

If only you knew...

"So, what's in it for you? Like, what do you want to get out of all this? 'Cause sitting in a car watching a bunch of guys trespass on someone's front lawn doesn't seem very appealing to me anymore."

Kit takes another contemplative drag. "It's exciting though. Don't you like the rush? You know there's something inside you calling you to it."

I tense up. *If you only knew...* "Why do you say that? Does something call to you?" I inquire.

She giggles again. "Being around Dan does."

"Ooooohhh," I tease. "The truth comes out!"

A pink hue floods her cheeks, almost matching the watermelon shade on her glossy lips. Her blue eyes get all twinkly in the shadows of the car. She rolls her head in my direction. "It would be cool if it were you," she coos, and my heart stops for a split second.

Me? Me what?

I grab her right hand and hold it tightly. "Um, Kit... you're like my best friend and I love you and all, but..."

Her lips hold her cigarette in place as she reaches over with her left hand and closed fist punches my leg. "You're such a dweeb, Joeph!" she tries to mumble, and stray ashes spray up onto the steering wheel. She swats them away onto the floor then flicks her cigarette out of the window. I can't help but laugh as I take a final drag and do the same.

"Seriously, what do you mean: it should be me?"

"You should be the leader. The Knights. It would be super cool. Like, you would make it all mysterious and serious and shit. Like the total opposite of what Ricky does, and…" She pauses and squeezes my hand. A gray light washes over her face in the shadows of the car like she's being bathed in the absent light of the new moon. She rolls her head again and looks over at me. There's a sadness and an odd spark in her blue eyes—even in the darkness I see her pleading look like a moment of clarity shining through and piercing my heart. "You're so different from anyone I've ever known, Joephie. Special. You're a good person."

"You really don't know," I whisper.

"I do know. I know you. I see you. You're my bestest friend in the whole wide world, Joephie Doephie!" She giggles and squeezes my hand tighter. "I'd follow you to hell. And that's why it *should* be you."

Movement from the bushes on Ocean Avenue stops her train of thought and doesn't allow me the opportunity to contemplate or respond to what she said.

"Shhh…" she whispers. "I think they're here."

"Look," I say, pointing to the right at the three figures heading down Ocean Avenue toward the house, "here come Seth, Thomas, and Dan."

"Wait!" she exclaims. "Look at the bushes next to the murder house. There's a light coming from there."

Next to the front lawn of the Amityville Horror house, candlelight shimmers from behind the tall shrubs. Someone's there. My muscles tighten up and a spasm shoots up my back. "Ricky?"

"Yeah, and one of his other goons, I think. I don't know who for sure. Could be some dude, Al or Jeff. Dan mentioned it before to me, but I wasn't really paying attention. I have no clue."

Ah, so the Acid King is here in the flesh.

I sit up at attention as the boys walk past our car on the opposite side of the street and disappear into the bushes with the others. More candle lights pop up and the greenery sways a little bit.

"Did you see Seth was carrying a big kitchen knife?" Kit says with a hint of worry in her voice.

Yes. I saw that.

But the words never leave my mouth. I'm too focused on the scene unfolding before me. Kit rolls down her window a little more so that we can hear what's happening across the street. The lights from the votive candles cast shadows in between the branches, like hundreds of arms reaching out onto the front lawn of the Horror House. Long, branchy hands with gnarled fingers point and beckon me to join them.

But I can't. I'm stuck here in this Chevy with Kit. *But it should be you.*

I lean forward and squint my eyes to try to make sense of the shapes transforming on the lawn. Images of body parts and monstrous figures manifest on the side patch of grass, and the shadows rotate in a swift circular motion that dizzies me, nearly hypnotizes me.

"They're so gonna get caught," Kit says with finality. "We're so gonna get in trouble."

They're casting the circle.

Echoes of chanting are carried on the wind. Latin, I think, but I'm not sure.

Open.

One of the boys holds up an object wrapped in raggedy brown cloth, and the humming and mumming gets louder.

"Holy shit, Joephie! They've got the hand!"

My chest tightens at the sight of it, like I'm struggling to breathe. Like, I can't catch a full and complete breath. Like, I'm kinda pissed that these fuckers are actually going to do something. I want to see! I want to see what they're doing!

But I can see...

In the space above the candlelight, in a place between a hanging tree, just in line with where they are behind the bushes, my eye catches a flicker. If I had blinked, I would have missed it, but I saw it plain as day. The air shifted, flickered, and spasmed right in time with a lightning jolt to my body that broke me out of that weird, hypnotic trance. A tiny rip in the space above them, like something trying to break through, or break in.

"Do you see that?" I say, mesmerized, and I'm not sure if I'm actually directing that to Kit or myself.

"See what?"

The rip glimmers and shimmers and slowly expands like a mouth creeping into a smile.

"Joephie? Are you okay?"

The boys' chanting gets louder.

Yes. Yes. I'm fine.

But then, a light from the house turns on, and the boys scatter in all different directions. I blink my eyes a few times, and the rip is gone. Like, poof. Disappeared.

"Holy shit!" Kit screams as she starts up the car. "Fuck! We gotta go! Now!"

Before Kit can peel away, the boy I don't know races up to my side of the car. His shaggy hair is a mess around his face and his eyes are wide and wild, like he's purely insane, possessed, or really, *really* high on something. *Maybe all three?* He slams his left hand against the car window, revealing a giant gash at his wrist. The blood smears all over the glass in slick streaks and he laughs a maniacal laugh.

"Kit," I urge from the corner of my mouth, "you can get the fuck out of here any time you like."

"I… I… I don't wanna run over his feet, Joeph!"

The boy tilts his head, extends his long, thick tongue and licks up the side of the window. He rolls his nose in the streak of blood making all kinds of swirly red designs for my entertainment. "Say you love Satan," he moans to me.

"What?" Kit screams as she slightly turns the wheel.

"I need you to say you love Satan," he repeats with that same, low voice—one that is obviously still deepening into manhood.

"Why?" I inquire. "Why do you need us to say that?"

"Ricky demands it! We all have to say it! All of the Knights!"

But it should be you. It should be me.

"Get the fuck outta here!" I yell. "Ricky can go choke on his own blood before I *have* to declare that to anyone."

With one more wheel turn, Kit screeches out of the spot on South Ireland Place and hangs a left down Ocean Avenue. "What the hell, man?" she breathes heavily when we pass the Horror House.

"Well, guess we're *really* not in the Knights of the Black Circle now," I joke.

"Guess not. I don't see how we can be."

"Fuck the Knights. Fuck those druggie assholes. And most of all, fuck Ricky Kasso."

Chapter 6

Thursday, May 10th 1984
First Northport Assembly of God
Northport, Long Island, New York
Night of the Waxing Gibbous Moon

I guess I'm cataloging my experiences here in Northport as "incidents." School is like, whatever. Stuff at home with Mom is the usual. I come to youth group and hang with my friends (if that's what you call them), we go to the sump and smoke up, talk shit, and do usual teenager stuff, so there's nothing exciting there or whatever. But I have "incidents." Moments of *feeling, knowing,* and *experiencing*—and *not* like your usual teenage stuff. Some teachers have been telling us that senior year is a year of self-discovery and growth. A lot of my peers are looking to leave home and go off to college, start their lives, prepare for their careers, marry their sweethearts, start a family, and blah, blah, blah. But I know I'm on a very different path of self-discovery. I'm experiencing a very different type of growth.

After the "Walpurgis Night Incident," I haven't been feeling so good. I had managed to get myself to school the rest of the week, but I skipped youth group last Thursday and hid away from everyone over the weekend. I took this Monday through Thursday off from school so that I could ride out this bug—a persistent migraine, a little nausea, and the feeling of an elephant sitting on my chest. No fever. No cough. Just tightness and a little shortness of breath. Enough to make me not feel like myself. And I actually would have been okay with all of that stuff, but the headache! Good Lord! There were times when I couldn't even stand up from my bed. My mother said to "sleep it off" and "rest," but when I did, I would have crazy, terrifying dreams with surreal images and sounds that were almost too real to be dreams. The noises were so loud inside my ears—like a hundred voices yelling at me at once—and whenever I closed my eyes, I saw red spots flickering behind my eyelids, so I tried avoiding sleep as much as I could, but that, in turn, exacerbated my overall feeling of icky. I was screwed either way.

Tonight is the first time I'm seeing everyone since school last Friday. I mean, I talked to Kit on the phone and everything, but I've been in a kind of self-quarantine. I plan on going back to school tomorrow because I've already missed so much. But whatever. Do I *really* care about that? Anyway, Thomas and Carmen are apparently *over*, over. And after Kit's admission of her undying love for Dan on Walpurgis Night, they finally got together and consummated their relationship. Love on Kit's part, lust on Dan's. I don't think he cares either way who is underneath him. Honestly, I don't think Kit is particularly Dan's type, but when all of your guy friends are talking nasty about the girls they want to hook up with and are binging on a steady diet of weed, Satan, and pornography, it's kinda hard to walk away from a willing pair of opened legs. I suspect this won't end well, especially since Dan is Kit's first, and she's obviously deeply invested in him.

Trent's voice booms in the church, which doesn't help my lingering headache. The sermon tonight is all about coveting—coveting your neighbor's possessions, coveting another's relationship, and even coveting another's social status—which is a concept I actually have never given much thought to. But when I contemplate Trent's words, it kinda clicks. Like, I can relate it directly to the Knights of the Black Circle and the assholes who flock to that scene. Kit said Ricky was a legend. And whether that "legendary" status is one of good or evil, it still elevates him to a position of power (whatever type of power that may be). Guys like Seth, Thomas, and Dan create these silly fraternities surrounding a person in charge because they want to be part of that power. They want to feel like they have some kind of influence or control over something—anything! Because their life is just one big, giant pit of self-loathing and...

"And next week, my friends," Trent's voice cuts into my thoughts, "we'll talk about self-worth and self-confidence, and how we, as a family unit, can lift each other up and hold ourselves to higher, more respectable standards." When he finishes his sentence, he looks directly at me. *Did he just read my mind? How in the hell did he know what I was thinking and connect it to the sermon?* A shiver runs through me, and I quickly look down at my boots because his eyes freak me out. He gives me creepy, creep-o vibes to the max. "So, we're at the mid-point of the night. Let's say we take a ten-minute break. When we come back, we'll finish up with some devotionals and accolades and our usual roundtable. Help yourself to some refreshments, use the restrooms, go smoke your cigarettes outside—although you know I don't approve of that." He chuckles, and the congregation returns the sentiment. "See ya back in the circle in ten, people."

Everyone stands up and filters throughout the room. The crew gravitates to the archway by the front door, and I feel Trent's eyes following us across the room. *Following me.* I tilt my head to the side to keep him in my sight. He's over by the refreshment table, and he makes it look like he's looking at the plastic cups of fruit punch, but his eyes are fixed on me. I glance up and away, and up again at him, and each time the expression on his face changes, like it's a kaleidoscope in constant motion. It's haunting and beautiful at the same time.

I reach the others at the front door, my back to the congregation. "Why is Trent watching us?" I whisper to Kit.

She shrugs and peeks her head over my shoulder. "Hmmm. I don't see him."

My eyes widen. "No, he's over at the snack table. He's just like, staring at us all weird-like."

She tilts her head to have another look. "Joephie, he's not even in the room. Are you sure you're feeling okay? Maybe you're still sick."

"I'm fine," I mutter, but I'm a little creeped out. I know he was watching and…

"Yeah, Joeph," Thomas teases in his obnoxious voice. "You sure you're feeling okay?"

"Yeah, yeah," I reply unenthusiastically.

Seth pulls out a cigarette from the front pocket of his jeans jacket. "What, were you sick or something?"

"Yeah. Just a bug. I'm okay now."

"Something must be going around. Ya know Ricky's been sick," Thomas says.

My ears perk up. "Oh, yeah? I didn't know," I try to say casually. I don't want to sound like I'm super interested in his well-being, but there's a part of me that's *super* interested in his well-being.

Dan tosses Seth a lighter. "Yeah. He got real sick right after Walpurgis Night. Pneumonia or something. His parents put him into the hospital 'cause it was so bad. Someone said he was coughing up blood!"

Ricky can go choke on his own blood…

"Wow," I reply. "That's fucked up."

"Totally," Kit parrots.

"So, we staying for the second half of this shit, or are we bailing?" Seth says, lighting up.

"Well, we obviously can't stay in here if you guys are smoking!" Kit declares.

I turn to look back at the congregation, to look for Trent's circus sideshow visage, but like Kit said, he's not there. A dull pain throbs at the base of my skull, and I nod. "Yeah. Let's go."

Seth pats his jean jacket pocket and almost crushes his pack of cigarettes. "Sump? I got two joints with our names on them."

Everyone agrees, and we head out the door. I look back one last time to see if Trent is back. He's not, yet I can still feel his eyes burning holes in me.

We all sit in a circle in a swath of grass, and Seth lights up one of the joints. He takes a drag and passes it to his left to Dan. "I *love* getting high," he croons. "I just love it. Is there anything better than mellowing out like this?"

"Oh yeah!" Dan tokes the joint and passes it along to Kit. She gingerly grips it in her fingers and takes a light puff. Dan blows his smoke directly in her face, and she gives a sweet giggle. A schoolgirl giggle. An I'm-so-gonna-have-sex-with-you-tonight giggle, but I don't think he notices or gets it.

Kit passes to me. I partake and send it to Thomas who's next to me.

"You guys ever have pot brownies?" Thomas says before inhaling.

"Pot brownies?" Kit asks. "Like, brownies made with actual weed?"

Thomas gives the joint back to Seth. "Oh man! You don't even know. My cousin upstate made them for us this one time. So good," he gushes in the memory.

"Sounds like they would be," Dan says. "Hey Joephie, your mom's cookies! Dude, with a little bit of THC, they would *really* hit the spot!"

"Joephie, your mom makes pot cookies?" Seth asks. His eyes are already glazed over with fucked-up-ness. *Lightweight.*

"Dude! Tell her to make us some!" Thomas slurs.

"They would be the best pot cookies in the world!" Dan chimes.

"On the planet!" Kit adds as she leans her body lovingly onto Dan's shoulder.

"In the universe!" Seth and Thomas say simultaneously. They stop for a second, look at each other, and burst into a fit of laughter.

I bend my upper torso over my crossed legs and my face twists in disbelief. "Nooooo," I whine. "My mother would never *dream* to make pot cookies!" I wave my hand in the air and "phuusshhh" my mouth as if I am imitating a horse. I rock my body back and suddenly realize, *Wait… I'm kinda fucked up too. After one hit?*

The joint goes around the circle again, and after my second pull, I really feel the effects of it. Thank God that I have the ability to know the limit is "now," so on the third pass, I put my hands up and let Kit hand it over to Thomas. I've lost track of how many times everyone has hit it up. That seems so secondary when I'm feeling like I've lost track of myself. That doesn't even make sense, but as soon as my thoughts form, they fly away into the air like burnt leaves disintegrating in the wind. I have a hard time catching them and putting them back together.

"Can I tell you guys a secret?" Seth says with his eyes closed.

Thomas claps a hand on his knee. "Anything man," he says very seriously. "We love you. Your secret is totally safe with us."

We all nod our heads in harmony.

Seth throws his hand up in the air and moves it in an arch above his head. A rainbow forms over him, shining a kaleidoscope light of multicolors onto his face. I blink twice. One. Two. It's not really there, is it? "This pot is the *best!*"

We all mumble in agreement.

"You know why it's the best, guys?" he continues.

Why? We all ask. We need to know. Our minds need to know the secrets of the universe! Please!

"Because I got it from Trent. But you can't say anything. You can't tell him I told you. I always buy weed from him, but he said this was special. And he was right!"

Everyone is quiet for about an hour, or rather, what feels like an hour, but when I look at us in the circle, we all sway our heads to some unheard song. Back and forth, back and forth. Hair swishing at our shoulders and backs. The energy of the

Earth propelling us from side to side. I can't hear the music, but I know it's there. I hear the music, but I know it's not really there. I feel the music because it's in my head, in the ground, and in the sky. We're all smiling at each other—wide, goofy-toothed smiles that indicate to each other our specific levels of "high." Kit smiles, wide but soft. No teeth to show, just a grin of glossy lips swept across her face. She puts a hand on my crisscrossed knee, and we stare at each other deeply. I fall into her eyes like blue cotton candy at a circus that makes me feel all sticky and sweet on the inside. *I wonder if her lips taste like bubblegum?* I think, and I feel myself inch closer to her.

"Dude, I think Kit's gonna kiss Joephie," Dan says, his eyes barely opened.

Kit immediately removes her hand from my knee and swivels her body to face him directly. "No, stupid. I'm gonna kiss you," she says before swallowing his face.

Dan pulls back a little, (like he's shocked? disgusted?) and the smacking noise of their lips sounds like a gunshot echoing in the night.

"Aww yeah," Thomas sings, cheering them on.

Kit rises and moves in front of Dan. She extends her arms to him, beckoning him to stand up and join her. Seth and Thomas hoot and holler as Dan gets up. "Relax, man! Relax!" Thomas shouts.

Kit licks her bubblegum lips. "Oh, don't worry. I'll relax him alright!"

More squeals and laughter from the boys. Kit grabs Dan's hand and leads him away from our circle and into the surrounding wooded area of the sump.

I lay back into the grass with my knees bent to the sky and I try to listen for the music again. How long have we been out here? A million years? A million seconds? The stars haven't moved. Thomas rolls over on his side and snuggles up to my shoulder. He sweeps my black hair away from my forehead and drapes it behind my head like an ebony carpet strewn upon the dark green grass. "It's so long," he marvels as he pets me with long stroking motions. I think I respond in my head, but I'm not sure. I continue to stare at the night sky, watching the stars, waiting for them to shift while Thomas brushes my hair with his fingertips like I'm a goddess being worshipped.

"The stars haven't moved," I declare. "Why haven't they moved?"

He pets my cheek. "I don't know," he says calmly. "Wanna go into the woods?"

I think I know what he means, but I know it's not supposed to be him. I know I will need more than five minutes, so I shake my head.

He jumps up angrily and runs his hand through his hair. I quickly sit up, pulling my knees to my chest. I feel my high knocked down a level when I meet Thomas's desperate eyes. My body floats back into itself, and I regain some of my conscious focus. "Why not? What are you, like a fucking dyke or something?" he screams at me.

"Hey! Hey!" Seth yells back in my defense.

Thomas swivels his head in Seth's direction and exhales loudly. "Fuck it! I'm going to take a piss!" And he stalks off into the woods.

Seth slides over to me in the grass, and I "phew" out loud. "What in the hell was *that* about?"

"Well, Joephie, isn't it obvious that he likes you?"

"Yeah, well, that doesn't mean I'm just gonna up and screw him!"

"Because you're a dyke?"

"What? No!" I squeal.

"I mean, you don't go with anyone. You're super close with Kit. You just turned Thomas down…"

My eyes narrow. "Sttttaaaahhhhppp!"

"Oh. I get it. You're a virgin."

I stiffen my back upright and pull my knees in tighter. "That's really none of your business, ya know," I snap.

He puts his hands up defensively. "Sorry, sorry," he apologizes. "Just trying to figure you out." He gazes at me with a caring expression. A light flickers behind his head—it's red, purple, yellow, and blue. Flashes, really. Like a rainbow being turned on and off with a light switch.

I shake my head to rid myself of the image.

"You okay?" he asks and his eyes are so gentle and serene, like green waves licking up the sandy beach. Like Kit's, I feel so drawn to them, drawn into them.

"Yeah, just coming down, I suppose."

He taps his jean jacket pocket. "Wanna go back up? I have one more joint left."

I huff out a little laugh. "Nah, nah. I'm good for tonight. That was pretty intense stuff, though. Are you still…?"

"A little. Definitely not like before, but enough."

"You really get this stuff from Trent?"

He breathes in heavily, contemplatively. "Yeah," he says softly. "Please don't say…"

"Promise," I cut him off. "Secret is safe with me."

"Thanks," he says, and he scooches an inch closer to me. "I knew I could trust you." He reaches over and gently strokes the top of my hand.

His touch is electric, and I tense up for a second. My heart thuds hard in my chest like it's about to burst out of me with a bloody splat. Maybe I'm not fully recovered from my high like I had thought. "I'm sorry you weren't able to find what you were looking for at the séance that night," I say after a moment, trying to divert his attention to me. *Or my attention to him.*

He moves his hand up my arm and goose-bumps spring up on my skin. "It's okay."

"I'm sorry if you got scared at that message. Seth's Death."

"Why would you be sorry?" He breathes closer into my neck. "It's not your fault."

My stomach quivers at his close proximity. "I know, I just…" And before I can say anything else, he tilts his head slightly and leans in. Our lips lock in an instant, as his tongue dances slowly and methodically with mine.

I swoon to the rhythm of his kiss—slow and gentle at first, our heads moving side to side in perfect coordination. Right side, right side, left side, left side. Back and forth in a swirling kiss of ecstasy. It tingles every last one of my senses and I am filled with the here and now—the nowhere—the scent in the air, Seth's smoky breath, the increasing fervor of his kisses, his one hand guiding me to lay back down in the grass and his other creeping its way up my shirt and underneath my bra. A wave of pleasure shocks me when he grips my nipple between his fingers and squeezes tight. I let out a soft squeak, indicating to him not to stop.

An overwhelming energy surrounds my body, much like it did the night of the séance, and I imagine myself levitating off the ground with Seth to the side of me, pleasuring my physical form.

Seth moves his head from my mouth to my neck, scraping his teeth gently up and down my clavicle and upper chest. His fingers release their hold on my breast, and he inches his hand to my miniskirt, pulls it up onto my stomach, and dips his hand into the heart of my panties. He probes me softly, feeling his way around my terrain like a blind explorer on an important mission. His fingers trace the outline of every inch of me, and the energy builds, bubbles, and boils over. I slip my hand down and shimmy my panties to my knees. With his fore and middle fingers, he grabs onto the soft flesh and rocks it gently back and forth, back and forth, like a ship rocking with the waves on the ocean. I gasp from the pleasure, arch my back, and rock my hips in time with his movements. I can't help but close my eyes and moan.

And the energy rises…

Just when I think I'm going to shoot up from the ground and into the sky like a rocket, Seth stops and inserts one finger gently inside me. I shudder at his touch, at the motion. In and out, in and out. It's relaxing and gentle and sweet all at the same time. He grinds himself against my thigh—his organ throbs through his jeans, but he's focused on pleasing me and not worried about his own needs.

My eyes roll in the back of my head in ecstasy, but something catches my attention, and I train my eyes to the night sky. "The stars moved!" I exclaim, but Seth continues to wriggle his finger into me.

And then I notice it—something in the sky, like a blob of clustered stars congealed together and spread apart forming a rip, a tear, a hole. Like the opening I saw above the circle on Walpurgis Night, but this is much smaller. I'm mesmerized by it. Stare at it. Want to reach my hand up into the night and pull it all the way open so that it can swallow me whole.

It'll swallow the world too, Joephie, a deep voice echoes in my head.

Seth kisses me hard again, but when he pulls back his head and my blurry, ecstatic vision comes into focus, for a split second, he's not Seth. His face goes jagged and pixelated, like I'm looking at him through a kaleidoscope. Like he's smiling with a circus clown Trent smile. *It'll swallow the world too,* the voice repeats from Seth's masked mouth.

Disturbed, I call out Trent's name, but Seth says something about the weed being the best ever, and it's him again—it's Seth's stoner voice back in my ear. My shoulders relax, and I ease up.

With every thrust of Seth's finger, with every soft moan I whimper out into the open air, the rip slightly grows larger. But this is not enough. I want it to happen now. I want to be swallowed and consumed and swept into that swirling energy, and I know exactly how to make that happen.

"You're not going to break me," I say to him.

Seth stops and says, "Okay," before lightly inserting a second finger inside me.

A breath hitches in my throat, not only from the pleasurable tingles in my body but also in anticipation for the tear in the sky to widen. But it doesn't.

I tighten the muscles of my sex around his fingers. He stops in his tracks and gives me a puzzled look.

"I said, you're not going to break me," I repeat, and his mouth nearly falls to the floor.

"R... really?" he stammers.

"Really," I assure him.

He takes a deep breath, and I hold mine, expecting the sky to burst open. He pauses for a split second then jams his fingers so deep inside me, I scream from the pleasure and the pain. My back arches higher, and yes, the hole in the sky slowly and steadily blooms wider like my insides, quickening with every thrust Seth delivers.

His fingers stab me so deeply, I can feel the tips of his knuckles hitting the base of me. My eyes flutter in ecstasy. My eyes flutter in agony. A red sheen sparkles behind my closed lids, and I envision the woods and the red, and the woods and the blood.

So much blood.

'Cause now it's not Seth stabbing my sex with his two fingers.

It's me stabbing Seth in the gut with a kitchen knife.

Seth's death.

Every plunge of his digits rocks my body with a vision of me plunging a knife deep inside him, returning the favor of sorts. I gut him from the inside out and play with his entrails, squishing them between my fingers, like he's squishing and jabbing the soft spots of *my* insides. I look down at my hands and see they are bloodied up to my arms.

But they're not really. I know they're not.

The rip in the sky pulsates at its edges, but it's not opening fast enough. Not eating me up fast enough.

Not killing him fast enough.

"Do you know how bad I want to fuck you?" he moans in my ear.

I grab his wrist and guide his fingers out of me, wiping them down on the inside of my thigh. A long trail of my honey glistens against my pale skin. Mesmerized, and speechless, he kneels before me, and pulls my underwear down around one leg so it dangles at my other ankle. He spreads my knees apart and stares at my exposed sex like a starved animal about to devour a long-awaited meal. I turn my head toward the sky and watch the ripple turn, pulse, and throb, and I know that the second Seth penetrates me, that *thing*, that… that *portal*, will surely burst open. I hear him unfasten his belt and unzip his jeans.

Get inside me already! I scream on the inside 'cause the suspense is maddening.

But it doesn't happen.

Thomas comes stumbling out of the woods and over to me and Seth.

Quickly, I sit up and reach down to pull my panties on, and Seth zips up his pants.

Thomas has a puzzled look on his face. "W… what the fuck, dude?" he yells to Seth.

Seth fishes for his belt in the grass, stands up, and loops it on his pants. "Dude," he tries to explain. "We were so fucked up; you don't even know."

I plop my body back down on the grass and loudly exhale an agitated sigh.

"Whatever, man. Whatever!" Thomas relents.

"Come on, let's find Dan and Kit and get the fuck outta here," Seth says. "Come on, Joephie. We're gonna go." He reaches his arm down to help me stand up. Before I take it and hoist up, I look at the sky one last time and see there's no more ripple, no more pulsing light, and the stars haven't moved a bit.

Chapter 7

Wednesday, June 6th 1984
Joephie's 18th Birthday
The Turner Residence
165 Harbor Hollow Road
Northport, Long Island, New York
Night of the Half Moon

I n the darkness, there is nothing but peace. It washes over me like a cold blanket and dulls my senses to the human world. The serenity of the great void carries my spirit to unknown places—uncharted territory. I know I should be afraid, but there's a song that repeats in my memory telling me not to be.

Be not afraid. I go before you, always…

I know I should be afraid of the voice too. It's gravelly, guttural, and in a language unknown to the human ear, unspoken on the human tongue, but it brews and twists inside me with clarity and an understanding only I can fathom. The voice guides me through the darkness—pushes and pulls me in every direction all at once, like chains hooking into my flesh and yanking me apart at the same time. There's a strange familiarity in this unfamiliar place, like I'm at the edge of time or the beginning of nothingness.

In the darkness, there is the absence of peace, and the longer I stay here, the faster it deadens my humanity.

Will I die if I stay here? I ask the voice.

You're already dead.

Sparkling lights like tiny stars begin to manifest in the darkness, and I watch the flashing little specks pop up all around me. The stars begin to move, to pulsate, like something on the outside of the darkness is pressing a hand down on them. Muffled voices echo in my blank space. A child speaks. I can't make out the words, but one rings true and clear—*Joephie*. I take a step back, but I'm afraid I'll fall into the void of nothing.

You are the nothing, the gravelly voice sings. *You are the everything.*

The stars shift their shape and collide in the darkness until they've collected themselves and expanded into the vast forest—the place I've been before with limbs made of bark dancing with the wind. They point their long, branchy arms at me inviting me to join them in their dance, but blood drenches the wood and pools at the base of the trunks.

The forest disintegrates into itself, leaving behind a small tear in the void. I know this ripple. I know this pulsating tear in the sky. I take a step forward and reach my arm out to touch it.

The closer I get to it, the wider it opens for me, revealing a pure light on the other side. It's warm and golden, and screams to me like a thousand voices crying out in agony. The warmth and the sound fill me with terror, but I'm not afraid, I'm not afraid, I'm not afraid—for there is beauty in the darkness, and monsters in the darkness, and light in the darkness, and peace in the darkness, and torment in the darkness...

You are the darkness.

The portal gapes wider, and I'm able to push my arm through it. An electric shock shoots up through me, and the light screams to me in a high-pitched wail, like a siren blasting off in the distance getting louder and louder.

You can wake up now, Joephie.

No. I'm almost there. Let me swim in the light.

Wake up now, Joephie.

Just. One. More. Minute.

Wake.

My body jolts awake from the dream to the sound of my phone ringing. Strands of my hair are caked to the side of my mouth with dried drool. My arm tingles with the numbing sensation of pins and needles, but I manage to heave my upper body over to grab it.

"Hello?" I ask with a crackly voice.

"Hey, birthday girl!" the baby-doll voice cheerily responds on the other end.

"Kit? What's up? Everything okay?" I croak, my vocal cords still adjusting to being awake.

"Uh, yeah! Everything okay with *you*? What, were you sleeping or something? It's nine o'clock at night!"

I rub the crusty corners of my eyes. "Yeah. I fell asleep when I got home from school. I passed out hard."

"Too much birthday partying?" she jokes.

"If Nancy's cookies are what you consider a party, then…"

Kit giggles, and the sweet sound of it rouses me from that confusing moment between sleep and awake. I can't help but smile.

"So, what's up?" I repeat, urging her to get to her point.

"Do I need a reason to call my best girl on her birthday?"

"Yes. Especially since you already wished me a happy birthday like a zillion times at school."

Kit pauses for a moment. The dead silence on her end forces me to exhale and close my eyes. I know something is bothering her, and sometimes with Kit, it takes some probing and investigating for her to open up. I just don't have the clear head for that now though.

"What are we going to do after graduation?" she says nonchalantly. But it's her cover-up statement, like the warm-up before she gets to the heart of the matter. Typical Kit conversation style.

"Seventeen days can't come fast enough, girl. We should figure something out. I'm all ears."

"Do you think your mom will throw you a party?" she asks.

"Psssshhhh," I exhale dismissively. "Seriously? I barely got a 'happy birthday' out of her today. I'll be lucky if she gives me a 'congrats.' Are your parents doing something for you?"

"Nah. I told them not to. I told them to just give me the money for vacation. Speaking of, we still need to work that out."

"Okay," I say flatly 'cause, honestly, that's the last thing on my mind.

"I was thinking ... being that Thomas probably won't have the money to go away *away*..."

"Me neither," I interject.

She ignores my comment. "Well, what if we could just use Seth's parent's house in the Hamptons for a week or like a weekend? They wouldn't charge us, you think?"

"I dunno," I mumble. "That would have to be a conversation to have with Seth."

"Well..." she sings, "speaking of..."

"Oh hush, you!" I scold. "Don't even start with me."

"C'mon, Joephie! It's been like, what? A month since you hooked up with him?"

"I shoulda never told you," I mutter.

"Why?" she squeals. "I'm sooooo glad you told me!"

"Stop. Just stop, please."

"Seriously? He's sooooo into you, Joeph. Like, constantly staring at you at youth. I know he calls you and stuff."

"Yeah, and I talk to him like a human being when he calls. I'm not weird to him at youth or when we hang out. So, what's your deal? Are you his mouthpiece or something?" I bark.

"No, I'm *your* voice of fucking reason, sister. Okay, okay, you had this really weird, really awkward, drug induced thing out in the great outdoors. Get over it! The awkwardness, I mean. I mean, d'uh, we've all been there."

"Yeah, Kit, the only difference is Dan is your boyfriend, and Seth was just a hookup." I rub my temple. This conversation with Kit is starting to spin in circles and it's giving me a headache.

Seth is the conduit.

A chill races through my lower body and I sit up straight, eyes fully open. "What did you just say?" I ask, slowly, trying to still find that voice in my head that was clearly not Kit's.

"I said, 'so Seth was just a hookup?'"

"I guess."

She huffs in frustration. Her breath makes a loud staticy noise in my ear. "All I'm saying is that he's superhot, you're superhot, he likes you like a ca-jillion, and I know you like him back. You've already jumped to the hookup part of your relationship—you might as well jump in the waters and see where this takes you. Could it hurt?"

"Did he put you up to this? He put you up to this, didn't he?"

"Nononono! I swear it! I'm just looking out for my girl 'cause I know you would do the same for me."

"Yeah, yeah. How is Dan, anyway?"

Another exasperated huff. "I don't know," she says, dragging her words out. "Tell me something, Joephie, and be honest with me."

"What? Anything."

"Do you think I'm hot? Like, for real hot. Like, if you were a guy, would you want me and shit?"

"You're crazy! You know you're a fox. A super fox."

"Okay," she says, her voice trailing. "So why doesn't Dan want me?"

"Why would you say that? You guys are like, together. Like, a couple. Why do you think he doesn't want you?"

"I don't know," she says dragging the words out again as if to preface something big and contemplative, but then she blurts, "Do you think Dan is gay?"

My eyes nearly bug out of my head, 'cause I have to admit, the thought had crossed my mind. "Has he given you any indication that he is gay?"

"I don't know," she repeats, defeated.

"Listen, all I know is if that asshole hurts you or breaks your heart, I will fucking kill him for sure. No one messes with my girl!"

Kit giggles, but it's a giggle through a stifled sob, and my heart kinda breaks for her. Suddenly, the front doorbell rings downstairs, and Kit sniffles, "Company?"

"I... I don't know," I stammer. I pull the phone away from my ear to listen to what's happening.

Mom's voice is shrill and fake as she tells the guest to hold on a sec and yells up, "Josephine! Seth is here to see you!"

Kit squeals on the other line and I *shush* her. "Oooooo, it's your sump-luvah!"

She's in full-blown hysterics when I say, "Shut the fuck up! I'll call you later!" and hang up. I get up and race downstairs to the front door as fast as I can so that I can do damage control before mom gets all nutty.

Just as I suspected, she's holding the tray of her chocolate chip cookies and practically shoving them in Seth's face. "Oh here, dear, this is Josephine's favorite."

"Thank you, Mrs. Turner," he says, taking one off the plate.

"Call me Nancy!" she gushes.

Quickly, I squeeze between my mother with the tray and Seth. He and I are practically nose to nose, and he says a small, "Hey."

I smile. "Hey." I think I even blush. Goddamnit! I'm such a dork!

"Can we talk?" he asks quietly.

"Come on, let's go," I say. He pops the cookie into his mouth, probably to avoid having to say anything else to my mom. "Be back later, Mom." And with that, we hop off the front steps and walk over to sit in his car parked across the street.

"Your mom totally makes killer cookies!" he exclaims through a mouthful of crumbs.

I roll my eyes and shake my head. "So I've been told."

He swallows hard and looks me directly in the eyes. "Happy birthday, Joephie."

I suck my lower lip with a squeaky sound. "Thanks. So, what's up?" I'm trying to keep my calm and collected, bad-ass rocker chick façade, but his eyes! I feel like a stupid girl crushing on the hot guy at school, and I hate feeling like this. Feeling vulnerable. Especially after what he and I did.

Seth is the bridge.

He says something at the exact same time as that gravelly voice in my head—that voice from my dream—and I screw my face up with a "huh?"

"I don't know," he says shifting in the driver's seat. "We haven't really talked since, ya know, a few weeks ago. And I'm still not sure about what really happened because Trent's weed was just so..."

"Unbelievable?" I offer, drifting back to the memory of that night and the memory of how I felt.

"Yeah. Exactly," he says, and I get the feeling he's thinking of that night, too. "Thomas was so pissed at me when he walked up on us. I mean, I didn't realize he liked you so hardcore. If I woulda known..."

"Fuck Thomas!"

Seth and I both laugh. "Yeah. Fuck Thomas is right."

I lean back in the passenger seat and curl my legs up to my chest.

"I don't want things to be weird with us, Joephie."

Uh oh. The 'it's-not-you-it's-me. I-don't-want-to-ruin-our-friendship' speech. I tighten my grip on my upper arms so as to brace myself for the inevitable let-down.

"No. They're not," I say coolly.

He looks out into the distance and nods his head. The waxing half-moon hangs heavy in the clear sky, almost casting a half spotlight on his face through the windshield. He has such unnaturally long eyelashes. I don't know why I notice that at that moment. "So, are we okay?" he asks.

I nod back in rhythm with him, but I'm not exactly sure what he means. "Yep. We're a-okay."

After a few seconds, he turns to face me. "Is this okay?" he asks as he puts a hand on the top of my knee.

I eyeball him curiously, put my hand over his and slide my knees back in front of me so his hand now rests on my thigh. "Totally okay."

He inches closer, his hand sliding up my thigh and landing at the crevice between my legs. My whole body tenses up. "How about this? Is this cool?"

Before I get to process and plan a witty comeback, he leans in and kisses me deeply on the mouth. His tongue rotates in time with mine.

Quick and short. Quick and short. Slow and deep. Quick and short. Quick and short. Slow and deep. It's a pulsating rhythm, like something trying to inch its way out from behind that portal — from behind that tear surrounded by stars in the sky — trying to burst through the soft spots in my mouth and enter my very soul.

He grabs the back of my neck with his other hand and pulls me closer to him, and for a split second, everything turns red in my mind. Each tongue dance-step sends a vision of bloody flashes—the trees, the woods, the knife, Seth's entrails decorating the trunk of the tree, but I'm the trunk of the tree, and my feet are sticky with his blood. And the blood sings. And Seth screams. And the trees cover me in their branchy limbs. And I laugh and dance naked around a big black circle burnt in the grass.

I scarcely notice that I'm sitting in a car with Seth, my now officially un-official boyfriend, passionately making out.

I scarcely notice he's furiously rubbing me hard between my legs.

I scarcely notice I've inched my hands up under his shirt and am scraping my fingernails up and down his back.

When we finally stop, I dreamily say, "That was pretty cool," and open my eyes to see him smiling brightly at me.

He pulls back away from me, breaking our embrace. "So ... *us*?"

I nod again, knowingly. "Yeah. I guess, *us*."

"You know Thomas is really gonna be pissed now!" he jokes.

"Yeah, well, like I said ... 'fuck Thomas!'"

We both smile at each other again, but I have a feeling it's for very different reasons.

Chapter 8

Saturday, June 23rd 1984
Graduation Day
First Northport Assembly of God
Northport, Long Island, New York
Night of the Waning Crescent Moon

It's hard to believe that today is graduation day—the day when all of the stresses of the last four years of high school come barreling to a screeching halt. Kit and I attended our ceremony for Northport Prep this morning at 8:00 a.m. Dan, Thomas, and Seth had their graduation from Northport High at around 9:00 a.m., so our ceremonies overlapped with each other.

And just as I had suspected, my graduation was rather unceremonious. The red cap and gown, hearing "Josephine Mary Turner" over the PA system, awkwardly walking up onto the auditorium stage, getting a piece of paper from someone I barely knew to confirm that I successfully completed my course work and can now move on. I have no ties to that school, just like all the other schools I've attended over the years. So many teacher names, I can't even remember them all. I never stayed long enough in one place to ever develop that fabled and sacred student-teacher bond with any one of them. You know the one—the one where the dedicated and passionate teacher takes the loner kid under their wing and nurtures them not only in their academic life but also in their entire being. The one where the student later writes novels and dedicates them to that one special teacher for "making a real difference in my life," or they win some stupid anthropology award at some stupid museum banquet, and they canonize said teacher for being the "most impactful person in my life." Yeah. None of that for me. My mother saw to that. When the ceremony was over, mom did congratulate me, and we drove back home in silence.

This upcoming week is apparently going to be the week of celebrations and party hopping, so in order to circumvent a low turn-out for youth group next week, Trent organized this special Saturday meeting for us so that we could all get together and congratulate each other and blah, blah, blah. The ages of the group members vary, and we five are the seniors, so Trent wanted to make our send-off special. He knows none of us will return after today, so this is our farewell of sorts.

We're in our usual circle, Trent in the center gesticulating wildly like he normally does, but as a special added treat, Trent asked us to wear our graduation caps so that we can symbolically "graduate" youth group. So dumb, but we oblige. Kit and I sit awkwardly in our satin red hats, and the boys don their blue ones.

Before the meeting started, Thomas had pulled us aside and said he had something really big to tell us, like something totally huge. He seemed really jazzed about it, which was interesting to me because he's been moping around like a giant blob the last few weeks, so the five of us are just sitting here, knees bouncing in anticipation for Trent to end it, dismiss us, let us throw our caps in the air for one last "hurrah," give us pizza, and send us on our way.

"Most of you have been with me from the beginning, from when I first came to be pastor here at First Assembly, but some were here before me, isn't that right, Kit? Dan?"

They both nod.

"And some of you just recently joined our little family. Joephie, we're so glad that you have come into our lives in this way. You've been an integral piece to our spiritual puzzle."

I tighten my lips together and nod. Integral piece to our spiritual puzzle? What the hell is he talking about? I really haven't added anything to this group. I've really only been a bystander, a witness, an observer…

"All of us are witnesses. All of us are observers. Together. Here. In this chapel."

I freeze and look at Trent sharply as another dreadful feeling courses through me. It's the same feeling of uneasiness and creepiness that I've gotten from him pretty much on a weekly basis. I can't explain it. It's like pinpricks on the back of my neck, a low thud at the base of my skull, goosebumps up and down my arms. I once asked Kit if Trent freaked her out, and I think she misunderstood what I meant. She thought I was asking if he was a pedophile or something, and she cheerily swept that discussion under the carpet. But there had been a hesitation in her voice. I think she knew what I really meant. She had to. Kit has a darkness inside her that is burrowed so deep in her heart and in her soul, that I know she doesn't fully understand the extent of her capabilities. I have no idea why I'm thinking about this right now, but Trent looks at me with a confused expression, and for a split second, he is legitimately confused—like he was trying to scan my brain and came up empty—just a bagful of scattered and unconnected thoughts.

"And so, my friends, we congratulate the accomplishments and achievements of our senior members. May you look up to them and continue to walk down their paths of success. Kit, Dan, Thomas, Seth, Joephie, thank you for allowing us to be a part of your lives. Thank you for allowing me to guide you on your paths. Thank you for allowing me to open up doors inside you that you never imagined possible, to lead you on your spiritual journey. I hope I have been able to guide you through whatever darkness you've gone through in your lives. I hope I've been able to help guide you through this wicked forest called life and help you rip through those spiritual portals in your soul."

The others smile and nod, but I freeze again. His parting words are directed at me and me alone. His parting words are a message. *He knows me. He knows what I've seen.*

"And so, I leave you five with these final words. One last time for good measure. I hope they stay with you all the days of your life: keep your good thoughts flowing, and your actions to match." He smiles wide and the congregation explodes in applause and hoots and hollers. Thunderous echoes against the stone walls. Trent leads the five of us to the center of the circle with him as the others stand at their chairs applauding us in a standing ovation. He motions for us to remove our caps and throw them ceremoniously in the air. We do, and they fall in the center of our circle as the rest of the congregation goes crazy for us.

Trent stands with us and motions to clasp our hands together. "I'm so proud of you guys," he says, tugging hard on Seth and Kit but staring straight at me. "You've done so much. Accomplished so much. More than you can ever comprehend. This is the beginning. The true beginning of things to come." With one final tug, he lets go and walks over to a group of freshmen kids who have flocked to the pizza table.

The five of us take a step closer to each other in a kind of secret huddle. "So, are we fucking done with this place or what?" Thomas asks, and we all give a little chuckle.

"Come on, Thomas," Dan urges. "What the hell do you have to tell us?"

He raises an eyebrow. "Tell. And show." We all eyeball each other in the circle. "But not here! Wave your goodbyes, say thank you to the group, we have a party to go to."

"Thomas," Kit croons, "there's no par…"

"You bet your ass there is!" he says, cutting her off.

I lift my head from the huddle and throw my hand in the air. "Bye everyone! Thank you, Trent. We'll see you guys around!"

The other four follow suit, waving and chanting their goodbyes.

"Ohhhh," Trent says with a knowing smile. "Let the parties begin, I guess!"

"Something like that," Seth says with a small laugh.

"Okay guys!" Trent yells across the room. "Stay safe and be good! Don't be strangers. You know I'm always looking for peer counselors, moderators, and general help around the church. Keep your…" he begins, and the congregation finishes the rest.

We all hop into Thomas's car and he pulls away like a bat out of hell. Dan and Thomas ride up front, and I'm in the back, squished between Seth and Kit. Seth's right hand is on my left thigh, and Kit's left hand is on my right thigh. Kit's nails rub me gently up and down, while Seth digs his fingers into my flesh, massaging first my knee and working his way up. And it's like a double turn-on because it's so out of the blue, and unexpected (well, maybe expected from Seth), and my brain is trying to focus on what's going on here in the back seat with what Thomas is saying frantically in the front seat. It makes my head hurt.

"So," Thomas says in a frenzied tone. "Are you guys ready to see a dead body?"

"What?" Kit squeals and grabs tightly onto my knee.

Dan punches Thomas in the arm. "Dude! What are you talking about?"

"Ricky killed someone, man. He fucking mutilated him!"

I roll my eyes. *Why am I not surprised that Thomas is talking about Ricky? He's pretty much obsessed with him!*

"What? Who?" Seth practically screams in my ear.

"His friend Gary, that guy that stole some PCP, or something like that, from Ricky a few months back... well, they were at some party the other night—Tuesday or something. Anyway, after the party, Al, Jimmy, Ricky, and Gary go out to Aztakea Woods, and they do some like ritual and shit. And everything goes totally crazy! Ricky fucking goes nuts and stabs Gary like a bajillion times. Gouges out his eyes and shit. They dig this shallow grave and just throw his body in it and leave him there."

"No way!" Dan yells. "I heard Gary ran away ... *again*."

"Who told you this?" Seth asks. He tightens his grip on my thigh, but I don't think he realizes it.

"Dude," Thomas huffs. "It's true. Ricky has been taking people out there to show them the body."

I shake my head in disbelief. "And nobody's said anything? The police haven't figured this shit out yet? It's been like what, four days? And Ricky is *taking* people to *show* them the dead body? I don't buy it."

"Really, Joephie?" Thomas scolds. "Do you really think someone's ratting Ricky out? Would *you* rat Ricky out? You know what he can do!"

No. No, I don't know what he can do because as far as I know, he can't do much of anything except sell drugs and try to open up portals in the sky. Rat out Ricky? I don't give a rat's ass enough to rat him out.

"Well, Carmen heard from Bill, who heard from someone at Cold Spring Harbor High who actually went with Ricky to see the body. Said poor Gary was screaming for his mom! Ricky said to him, 'Say you love Satan!' and all Gary could say was 'No! I love my mom!'" Thomas laughs maniacally.

I remember the boy pounding on Kit's car with his bloodied hand and screaming something or other about declaring our love for Satan on Walpurgis Night. He had an insane gleam to his eyes. They were red like blood and sparkled with stars, but he wasn't a real boy. He wasn't a real person. He was something else inhabiting the form of a boy. Something hidden, dark, and not of this world. Like a switch had been turned off in his humanity and something else invaded his mortal space. I remember his voice—frantic and hysterical with the human voice, but below the timbre, it was gravelly and guttural, and to think on it now, that voice has spoken to me many, many times before.

I guess I get lost in my memory of that night because, before I know it, Thomas is pulling into the parking lot of the woods, and the car shuts off. Kit shakes my leg. "Joeph, we're here."

I rub my eyes. I guess I fell asleep, but I know I wasn't sleeping, if that makes any sense.

"It's about a ten-minute walk to the body," Thomas declares.

The summer sun begins to set, and I'm grateful for the approaching cover of darkness—like a blanket to shield us from intrusive human eyes, while at the same time, a veil pulled back so that the eyes of the forest can look out for us. *For me.*

Kit speeds up her gait and reaches Dan. She clasps her hand within his and rubs his arm with her free hand. "Are you sure you know where you're going?" she asks.

"Of course I do!" Thomas defends. "Carmen told me the exact location."

"Did Carmen actually see this body?" I ask sarcastically.

"Uhhh, no Joephie!" he responds with the same level of sarcasm and annoyance. "But I trust her. She knows what she's talking about."

I roll my eyes. "Yeah, yeah," I huff.

Seth throws an arm around my shoulder and pulls me into the crook of his arm. "Don't be scared. I'll protect you," he says with a soft smile.

"Since when do I need protecting?" I smile back.

Thomas leads us through the woods, talking incessantly about Ricky this and Ricky that. And Ricky's so hardcore. And Ricky's a badass. And Ricky's Satan's chosen one. And Ricky is the best leader of the Knights of the Black Circle. And Ricky can make shit happen at will. And Ricky blah, blah, blah. Thomas's loyalty and devotion to whatever cause this is for is super clear. He makes no concessions about his feelings for the Black Circle. Thomas is a disciple through and through. He keeps looking down to his hand and mumbling some shit to himself when I realize he has instructions written on his palm. Is he fucking for real? On his *palm?*

My irritation is at its apex, and I know I can't contain my disdain for this whole situation much longer. "I guess you're like a full-blown member and stuff," I say to Thomas, taunting him. "Because, ya know, you know secret shit now. More than Dan and Seth even."

Thomas stops and looks back at me with a sneer. "Just because I got some info on a dead body doesn't mean I'm 'in' yet." He looks quickly back and forth between Seth and Dan with an almost guilty expression, like he's hiding something. "We're all 'in' together. That hasn't changed." Thomas turns on his heel and pushes forward into the woods, but I've already planted the seed of tension among the three guys. I can feel it radiate in the space between Seth and Dan, and I can't help but smirk to myself on the inside.

A few minutes later, we reach a clutch of trees and Thomas announces, "We're here!" But "here" is so unassuming and inconspicuous in the gloaming. Thomas points to an area of disturbed tree branches and leaves surrounded by a column of flies. Their buzzing sound fills my head and makes me dizzy. "Look! There!" and he clenches his fist and points with his pointer finger more dramatically.

Dan walks over to the mess of leaves.

"Don't touch it!" Kit screams to him. There's a real sense of fear in her voice, a real heightened awareness, like she knows this isn't a game, or some parlor tricks, or some drug-induced sex-orgy. This is the real deal. There's actually a dead body in that makeshift grave and something inside her kinda freaks out.

Seth's shoulder muscle tenses up for a second, and I know he kinda feels the same way as Kit. They all do. They all have that same balance of curiosity, fear, disgust, wonder, and sadness. I can feel it come off of them like the heat coming off of the pavement on a summer night. It moves in waves, creating an aura of blurriness around their bodies. It's the manifestation of their confusion—*we shouldn't be here, we want to be here, we don't want to be here, we need to see, but we don't want to see.* They wrestle with each dilemma, back and forth, back and forth.

But not me.

I need to see it.

Dan kicks at the pile until we see a speck of clothes poke through—a jean jacket. Kit gasps in her throat with a cute, squeaky sound that makes me wanna sigh, "aww."

Thomas continues to sweep away the foliage with his foot. "Ricky said they made Gary take off his socks and cut off his jacket sleeves as a sacrifice to the fire 'cause their wood was too wet," he says matter-of-factly.

Seth leaves my side and goes over to help them. I follow behind him, but Kit puts out her arm to stop me. "Don't!" she pleads with a desperate look in her eye.

I grip her hand and put it back to her side. "It's okay," I coax. "I just want to have a look."

She stares at me like a frightened doe caught in the headlights. Her blue eyes go round, and I think they rim with tears, but I can't be sure. She remains frozen in her spot, and I move closer to Seth's side, examining the shallow grave as the boys remove layer after layer to reveal the unthinkable.

Gary's body.

But it's not really a body, per se. It's a hunk of meat. An unfinished dissection of flesh. A mass of unrecognizable decomposition.

"Jesus fucking Christ!" Dan exclaims. "What in the holy fuck is *that*?"

Seth takes a step back when a soft breeze wafts the smell of rot up his nostrils. "Dude! That's fucking rank!"

Actually, all three of them step backward, yet I move closer, unaffected by the smell, unfazed by the sight. I need to see it. I need to smell it. I need to hear the pattern of the flies as they hum around the open gashes of the once face. Another breeze blows by, carries the smell to my open mouth, and I taste it. I taste the decay on the roof of my mouth and the back of my throat. It tastes like suffering and a thousand screams. "He screamed a thousand times," I say out loud, but I don't think they hear me. I close my eyes, relax my body, and begin to feel a surge of energy come up from the pit of my stomach—that familiar feeling of levitating off the ground overwhelms me. I fall to my knees at the feet of the body and touch them.

"Joephie! No!" someone yells in the distance.

"Where are his eyes, man? What happened to his eyes?" someone else screams in horror.

But they sound so far away from me, I don't even acknowledge them. The buzzing of the flies drowns out their voices, anyway.

And when I open my eyes to look at the body before me, I see the portal, the opening, the tear in the sky right in the center of the tree line. It's there, but it's inactive. It doesn't pulsate, glow, or give any indication that the mouth of it is widening. It's frozen in time. Frozen in place, like it had started to open, but something stopped it in its tracks and it never got a chance to come to fruition. *It never got a chance to be born.* A crow flies onto one of the low hanging branches of the tree next to where the body lays. I look up at it, at its piercing, red eyes glowing in the twilight of the forest. Its black feathers shimmer iridescently, like an oil slick hitting the sunlight and reflecting back greens and yellows and browns and golds. Only there is no sunlight—just the refracting last shimmers of day fighting their way against the horizon and glinting off the crow's sacred shape. His eyes speak to me in a guttural voice. That same guttural voice that has been haunting me for weeks now. For months now. For my whole life somehow. The crow caws, and I am filled with peace.

Someone taps me on the shoulder, and in an instant, the humming of the flies quiets down. I quasi-snap back into reality and swivel my head around to see Kit and her worrisome face behind me. "We're going, Joephie." She puts out her arm to help me up, and I grab onto to her hand and hoist myself back to standing. I look back to the tree, but the crow has flown away.

The boys cover the body back up, trying to recreate what it looked like when we got there. "Are you afraid?" I ask her.

"No. Not really. I mean, it's weird as all get out, for sure. I'm more scared of getting into trouble over this, ya know?"

I nod. I understand what she means. The boys finish up, and we walk back to the car.

"I can't believe he really did it," Dan says with disbelief. "Ricky really killed Gary." Kit wraps her right arm around his waist, and he throws his left across her shoulders. They walk out of synch with each other through the uneven terrain of the forest.

"Yeah, man," Seth interjects, "like it's all fun and games..."

"Until Gary loses his eyes?" Thomas jokes.

"Not cool, man. Not cool," Seth finishes. "Seriously, the whole Knights thing... séances, grave digging, conjuring, getting fucked up—all of it is fun and shit, but I don't think I wanna sign up for murder."

"But it wasn't like *murder,* murder," Thomas defends.

"It was a sacrifice," I mumble, not realizing I said it out loud.

Seth nudges my arm. "It's still murder, though."

"Seth's right," Dan says. "Do we really wanna be tied in to all this?"

"Well, we are now. Like it or not, we all saw that dead body. We all know what happened. And we're all gonna keep our fucking mouths shut," Thomas scolds, throwing his hands wildly in the air.

"Yeah, yeah, yeah," Seth agrees. "For sure. I just don't think that..."

"We should have our own circle!" Kit interrupts. "Like just us!" She squeezes Dan's waist tighter.

"Fuck the Knights," I say under my breath.

"Yeah, like just us hanging out and shit," Dan agrees.

"Séances at Seth's," Kit gleams.

"Smoking out in my car," Dan adds.

"Or the sump..." Seth says as he eyes me slyly.

We all stop our walk for a second and give each other knowing glances. A wave of anger overtakes Thomas's face. "I don't know, man. I don't think it works that way."

"Says who?" I bark at him. "We're not bound in blood to anyone or anything. I never declared my allegiance to the Knights of the Black Circle. I never said I loved Satan. Fuck! I never even met the Acid King! Besides, we don't have much time left together 'cause I'm fucking out of here in a few weeks anyway, so who fucking cares?"

Kit reaches out and grabs my hand. "Wait! Joephie, what are you talking about?" she says slowly.

"What? You know I'm leaving this town. I've told you that since I got here."

A confused expression blossoms on her face, and it irritates me to no end. "Joeph, we're going to Suffolk Community College." She pauses. "We all are."

I look around at everyone. They all stare at me like I have a hundred faces, each with a different expression. "No. I'm not. I'm going out west for school. To start over. To get away from my mother."

She squeezes my hand. "Joephie," she begins slowly, "don't you remember the guidance counselor's seminar? We filled out that application. Remember they said that if we applied through them, they would waive the application fee? Remember we agreed that we would do two years at SCC to get all the pre-reqs out of the way?"

I narrow my eyes. I have no idea what she's talking about. "You're fucking with me, right?"

"No. I swear I'm not. *You're* fucking with *me*. Right?" She looks sad. Confused. Afraid. Afraid for me?

Afraid of me?

"Alright! Alright!" Seth intervenes, breaking up the weird vibe in the air. "It's been a long and strange day. Let's get Miss Josephine home. Bet you haven't eaten since this morning, right? You probably need some grub and rest." He swoops me by his side, pulls me close to him, and leads me out of the forest and into the car.

Chapter 9

Friday, July 6th 1984
First Northport Assembly of God
Northport, Long Island, New York
Evening of the Waxing Gibbous Moon

I'm not sure why, but for some reason, my mother has been on my case all week about my stupid graduation cap. Something about having a memento of my accomplishments and blah, blah, blah. "You don't have a yearbook. You didn't get a class ring. How are we going to remember this? I need some kind of physical reminder. I want to put it on the mantle with Grandma." Did she even stop to think that maybe I don't want to remember it? Maybe I don't want to have a physical reminder of the uneventful experience I had at Northport Prep. Maybe putting as much distance as possible between me and this whole godforsaken island is what I really want. Did she ever think of that? Nope. Never even crossed her pea-brain. But I swear if I had to hear "But your cap," one more friggin' time, I was going to slit her throat and dance in the fount of blood sprouting from her neck. I would have drunk it too, as a big "fuck you" to her and her need for nostalgia.

I wracked my brain continuously, trying to remember where the damn thing was. I searched my bedroom, my mother's car, our back yard (I don't know why—it just seemed like the thing to do at the time).

I walk over to Thomas's house to see if I could take a peek in the back seat of his car. He rubs the stubble on his chin and through the black screen door, his face looks speckled and splattered. "Jesus Christ, Joephie! Don't you remember? Trent had us do that stupid 'throw the cap' thing at youth, and we just all left them there. Trent probably has them."

I vaguely remember that. I guess, when something is so insignificant in the moment, it doesn't stick with you. I couldn't care less about it all, to be honest. "Okay, I'm gonna go over there now. Do you want me to get you yours if I see it?"

"Wait? You walked here and now you're gonna walk over there?"

"Uhhh … yeah. What's the big deal? I walk everywhere. You know I don't drive."

He squeezes out from behind the front door and stands practically nose to nose with me on the stoop. "Let me drive you over there."

His breath is smoky, like he'd recently smoked an entire pack of cigarettes, and I cringe on the inside for a split second at the thought of being alone with Thomas in his car. I don't know if he's still raw about me and Seth being together or what. It really doesn't even make sense because it's not like Thomas and I were ever a thing or even close to being a thing. I shrug off the feeling and say, "Sure."

We pull up to the church and Thomas shuts the car off. "I'll wait out here for you, okay?"

"Sure, no problem," I say and turn my upper body to open the door.

"Joephie, wait!" he calls.

I swivel back to face him. I widen my eyes, imploring him to say what he wanted me to wait for, but he doesn't say anything. He just stares at me, and I get that icky feeling again, like "c'mon man, say whatchoo gotta say."

"What's up?" I urge.

He huffs and stammers and makes this gross gurgly noise in his throat before fishing for a cigarette in his jeans pocket and lighting it up.

"You alright?" I ask, trying to get him to make some sort of verbal response.

"Yeah, yeah, yeah," he says with a breathy exhale. "Nothing. Forget it." But he's nervous. Ultra-fidgety.

"You sure? Did you wanna talk about something?" I want to punch my own face. I don't know why I opened that door, 'cause quite honestly, I don't really want to talk about anything with Thomas if it's going to be about him and me, or worse … Ricky, because Ricky was arrested yesterday and I know Thomas has got to be all upset over it.

"It's cool. It's cool. Just get your hat and hurry the fuck up, okay?"

"Sure thing," I say, and get out of the car.

I walk into the stillness of the church and the door squeaks with a creaky echo. In the front vestibule, Trent has a large cardboard box labeled "Lost and Found" and sure enough, poking from the top are the red and blue satin graduation caps. I walk over and start to take them out of the box. I know the others really don't care about them either, but I'm here, I might as well just get 'em for everyone, ya know, in case their mothers are all freaking out too.

I grab mine, and before I get a chance to pick up the others, I hear music coming from one of the back rooms. It's a strange song with a familiar timbre. No vocals, a guitar track, a piano track, drums, and some ambient shit flitting around the melody. It's almost like a heavy metal, new age fusion. It's interesting. Interesting enough to draw me in and make me wander around the insides of the chapel trying to locate the source.

The music grows louder and more intense as I approach the back office. The drum beat blasts like Slayer—hard and heavy and nerve splitting, but the lilting harmonies of the other light instruments are like fairy voices in the wind—uplifting and soothing like cough medicine on the back of a strep throat. I peek in the room to see Trent sitting at his desk poring over a pile of papers.

He looks up at me from narrowed eyes and smirks, like he knew I was coming. *Was he expecting me?* "Joephie!" he beams and turns the volume down on the cassette player on his desk. He stands up and motions for me to take a seat across from him.

"Oh, no…" I stammer. "I just came to get…"

"Yeah, you guys ran out of here so fast last week, you didn't even stop to take these with you, or stay long enough to have some food."

I kinda lower my head with an inkling of guilt. "Yeah, sorry about that."

He waves his hand in the air. "Stop! I get it! Places to go, people to see," but he says it in a way that sends a shiver up my spine. "Sit! Talk with me for a little."

"I… I really can't. Thomas is waiting for me in the car, and…"

"Please! Like you care what Thomas thinks. You know damn well Thomas will wait for you for however long you make him wait." He chuckles. It's infectious and inviting. And weird. And I can't help but answer his offer of a few minutes.

"I can stay a sec," I say as I sit down. He nods and joins me.

"So…" he exhales, "off to the great wide open, are we? The big bad world." He pauses and clasps his hands together on top of his desk. "You and I never really did get a chance to sit down and have a heart-to-heart, ya know. I feel like I've bonded with all the other members of the group, but you were always so elusive, so confined to your own space."

Because you're a weirdo.

"Well, being the new person kinda marked me as odd man out, ya know? Everything just happened so fast with my move and new school..."

A small frown of disappointment forms on his lips, and it makes me feel, I don't know, guilty? My heart starts to race, and I feel like I owe him an explanation of sorts, and I don't know why. I don't like feeling like this—like I'm in debt to someone, or I have to explain my actions to someone I barely know.

"But it's not like I didn't get anything out of youth," I blurt out, trying to cover for myself. The second the words come out of my mouth, I want to smack my forehead with my palm. *So stupid.*

"I understand," he says gently. "I know you did. If you got anything out of my sermons, it was the connection of friendship made right there in our weekly circles. I saw how you and Kit connected immediately. And Dan, Thomas, and Seth. You found your people here. They will serve you well."

I nod, but I find his choice of words a bit odd.

He shifts forward in his chair and a large, open smile invades his face. His white teeth seem to brighten up the space around him and illuminate against the calendar blotter and newspaper at his desk. It kinda freaks me out—the brightness of them against his unnaturally bronzed skin. It's like he's not even real. Not a real person. For a split second, I actually wonder if any of this is really happening. *Am I making this up? Is this a dream? A hallucination?*

"And moving forward? What's next for the great and mysterious Josephine Turner?" he asks, cutting into my thoughts.

The sound of his voice drags me away from wandering too far away in my mind. I quickly shake my head, focusing on the reality in front of me. "I'm gonna go out West. As far away from here as humanly possible. Kit seems to think I'm going to SCC with them, but I'm not. I can't. I just need to go."

"How far West?" he inquires.

"Cali. As far as the US map will take me without having to cross a body of water."

"I'm from California," he says.

"Oh, yeah?" I reply, unaware.

"Yep. And you should definitely give it a second thought. It's not everything it's cracked up to be."

Suddenly, I remember Dan saying something about Trent's past... *Yeah, he had a rough childhood and shit... He's like a reformed Manson cult member or something crazy like that.* I stare at Trent, trying to read his face, wondering if he'll elaborate on his personal story with me.

"Oh, I have nothing to hide, Joephie," he says, as if he's read my mind ... *again.* "It's no secret that when I was just about a few years younger than you are now, I was involved with some messed-up people. Did some messed-up things, but for all the wrong reasons. Everything was predicated on a lie, and I was lucky enough to get out of there while I still had the chance. There are a lot of false prophets in this world, Joephie, and it's very easy for a young person to fall prey to their wily charms."

Like lightning flashes in my brain, my body is rocked with strange and disturbing images. I can't seem to get a handle on what they were—a bloody knife, an open field with a mountain range in the background, a circle of people, what looks like a compound with a trailer and some run-down building on it. And screaming. Lots and lots of screaming. The quick flashes make my head pound and I stand up. I have to go. Have to get out of here. "Yeah," I say, trying to sound like I'm shrugging off his admonition but really trying to inconspicuously dismiss myself from his presence, "but I've kinda made up my mind though. As soon as I can, I need to leave this place."

He plants his palms on his desk and rises with me. "Do you, though? Don't you still have a lot to do here?" I look down and stare at his hands on the desk because my head hurts so badly, and I'm not sure if Trent actually spoke those words out loud.

"I... I should go," I stammer. "Thomas is gonna be pissed that I've been so long and..."

He walks over and stands beside me, but my eyes are still trained on his desktop. I notice the headline on the newspaper and read it upside down: "L.I. Cops Hunt Killer Cult." There's a picture of Ricky next to it. He's scowling at the camera, in handcuffs, in his AC/DC t-shirt, and for the first time ever, I get a really good look at his face, at his demeanor, at his complete and utter disregard for what's happening to him. There's not a shred of remorse or guilt behind his eyes, but I wonder if that's pure, stone-cold evil, or some drug-induced look. I mean, they don't call him The Acid King for nothing, ya know.

Trent watches me stare at the newspaper for a few moments before he reaches over and spins it around so I can see it right-side up. But right-side up, Ricky looks less menacing, and actually, pretty sad and pathetic. "They got him," Trent muses.

"I knew him," I say under my breath. "I mean, not personally. I knew *of* him. Through other people."

Trent nods his head and taps his thick forefinger on Ricky's face. "Such a shame with the Kasso boy. There was so much potential."

I breathe in and turn my head to face him, but he looks longingly at Ricky's front headline splash. I purse my lips together. "Yeah…" I start to say, thinking back to that one guidance counselor at my old school who sat me down and gave me the whole lecture about how life is a gift, every day is a new adventure, how being a kid is the worst and greatest time in your life, and to not waste your potential with frivolity. Blah, blah, blah.

"But the drugs," Trent continues, giving Ricky's picture a final tap. "The drugs rotted out his brain and made him lose his true focus."

He puts his hand on my shoulder, and I freeze. My insides go cold, like ice coursing through my veins. I think I actually shiver. I don't know. Every blonde hair on my arms stands at attention like hundreds of soldiers waiting for their battle commands. He lifts my chin so that I can meet his eyes. His fingers are blazing hot against my skin—in stark contrast to the layer of frost that encompasses my body. "Focus?" I croak, the word barely escaping my throat.

"Poor Gary suffered for nothing, and that's not right." His voice sings to my eyes. "The suffering needs to have an ultimate outcome or else it's just wasted screams in a vacuum. You know. You saw it. You *heard* it."

I close my eyes for a second. I see the spot in the Aztakea Woods with the inactive rip in the sky. I smell the rotting body—the corpse, the shell, the wasted sacrifice. I hear Gary screaming in the night, the waning moon not quite full, not quite half, bathing his bloody face.

He screamed a thousand times.

"Screams in the wind that amount to nothing." He tsks his teeth together with disappointment. "Such a waste. Such a shame." He moves his hand from my face and places both of them on my shoulders in a loving way. "There was so much hope for Ricky. But he was polluted. Unlike you, Joephie."

"My mother says I was cursed by a witch," I shamefully admit.

"No, Joephie. Not cursed. Blessed."

And in an instant, it all comes alive in Trent's eyes. We stare at each other for what seems like an eternity, but in our time, our gaze lasts all but a second. And in that second, he walks with me through burnt forests. Holds my hand. Points to the hanging bodies swinging by their necks from the tallest limbs of the tallest trees. Metal trees, with white cloth rope swung around the lattices, clutching tight to the distended necks of their victims, trying to keep their faces in place, but gravity proving otherwise. But the closer I look, I realize the bodies are really just one body belonging to the same person, screaming a thousand times for their faults, suffering for all eternity because of their mistakes. *Because he deserves it.*

There is fire in the distance, and the smoke fills my nostrils. The heat of the summer sun blazes through the layer of hazy smoke and penetrates my bare shoulders, kissing me with its flames. There is gritty ash on the ground, at my feet, and I bend down to touch it. It's fresh. Hot. Ashes of the bodies burned in my wake. I press my hands to the ash, driving my palms deep in the pile, grinding them into the dirt and mashing the ash and bone fragments into the pits and grooves of my palms. I raise my hands to my face and press them against my cheeks. I carry the dead with me.

"And may the souls of the faithful departed rest in peace," Trent says to me in that guttural voice—the voice I've known for so long—and he tells me ancient stories that span a thousand lifetimes. I know the words. I know their meaning. And underneath it all, there are instructions. Guidelines. He tells me I'm the vessel. I think I know what he means. I *know* I know what he means. At the deepest, innermost part of my core.

"It was always you," I mumble to him.

"No, it was always you," he answers.

Every weird vibe or feeling I've ever had about Trent melts away in the hazy sunlight. I am at peace in his presence because I can finally see. He has watched me from day one. Guided me to this moment. Our journey stops when he breaks our gaze, and he reaches to his cassette player, ejects the tape, and hands it to me. "Everyone is so consumed with this Satanic Panic; they wouldn't notice the real thing if it burned an X on their heads."

My head throbs again, and a giant red X flashes on Trent's forehead for a split second. And then it's gone.

I put the cassette in my pocket, clutch my stupid graduation cap, nod at Trent, and leave.

When I get back into Thomas's car, I'm a little dizzy.

"Hey," he says, emotionless.

"Hey," I say in a daze. "Sorry I took so long."

He looks at me strangely and puts his cigarette out. "Huh? You were like two minutes. It's fine. Get what you needed?"

"Yep," I say.

"Wanna go get something to eat?" he asks, starting up the car.

"No, just take me home. I'm not feeling so good."

Back home, Mom is baking cookies tonight. I'm not sure why, but the scent hangs heavy throughout the house. Before I join her in the kitchen, I walk through the living room and place my grad cap on the mantle next to Grandma Jane's urn.

"Did you get it?" Mom calls to me.

I roll my eyes and huff. "Yes, Mother! I put it right where you wanted it."

"Thank you!" she sings. "Why don't you come and help me in here? I have two more batches to do. I could use some extra hands."

Extra hands.

Extra ash-stained hands.

Extra ash-stained hands from burnt bodies with bone fragments caked underneath my nails.

Without even thinking about it, I open the cover of Grandma Jane's resting place and dip my fingers deep inside, pressing them down hard so that a layer of her remains coats my digits and collects beneath the darkness of my black painted nails. I do the left hand first, then the right. I hold my palms in front of my face and smile at her. I think she smiles back. "Coming!" I say, and I happily join my mother in the kitchen.

Chapter 10

Friday, July 13th 1984
The Turner Residence
Northport, Long Island, New York
Night of the Full Moon

R icky Kasso is dead.
On July 7th, the day after his arrest, he was found hanging in his jail cell.

I try hard to wrap my head around his suicide. What must have been going through his head to do that to himself? Guilt? Fear? Anger? I saw his pictures in the paper, and from my assessment, he didn't exhibit any of those things. Could it have been longing? Like, a peaceful calm to take him to the other side? Did he think he would be punished for his sins? Absolved? Did I have something to do with it? *Metal trees, with white cloth rope swung around the lattices, clutching tight to the distended necks of its victims, trying to keep their faces in place, but gravity proving otherwise.*

Since Ricky's death, I've heard the forest calling to me more clearly now. It screams my

name at night so loudly that I can barely drown out the sounds in my head. It's almost as if Ricky's passing opened up some sort of pathway that leads directly to me. When I close my eyes and try to sleep, the voice of the woods carries on the night wind and penetrates my brain. It's a dull ache that starts right above my eyes and shoots up through my forehead and travels down along the base of my spine. But it's not a pain like I would normally experience pain. It's almost like an invasion—a presence letting me know that it's with me, beside me, guiding me. I feel and hear it simultaneously. It makes me tingle and my skin crawl. My skin crawls so much that a few nights I've laid there in my bed scratching my arms to try to make it stop. I scratched so hard that I've torn open long, jagged track marks up and down the surface of the skin. I only realized I had bled when I woke up in the morning with brown blood stains on my sheets. But there was no pain, just sensation.

And I can hear Trent's voice too, but it's not really Trent's voice, ya know? I hear that guttural, bass-toned dirge in the center of my chest. It blends with the voices of the woods and sings to me a song of the ancients. It's strong, the song. Unlike any human heavy metal noise or pop culture radio jams. This song is pure. Real. Divine. I don't think it's meant for human ears to hear or to understand—like the backwards message in the Blodheksa song, it's something hidden and kept secret from the human mind because the human mind simply can't understand it. I think it's probably the first song ever to have been created in the cosmos. Like, written by God or something else.

Someone else.

Images of the dormant portal haunt me, raise my curiosity even higher. Every time that I've seen it start to spread its smile wide open, I was filled with the absolute and supreme sense of wonder and peace. I need to know what's on the other side. I need to *feel* what's on the other side. When Trent told me I was the vessel, I knew exactly what he meant—I am the one who needs to open that portal. He knows. He's seen it. I don't quite understand why he can't do it himself, maybe he doesn't even know. I get the feeling that he needs to have it open too. Like he needs to go home or something. I don't know what I'm even thinking right now. That's craziness.

But is it?

Because what isn't crazy is the song of the Aztakea Woods.

In my head.

Calling me to go there.

Calling me to cast a circle where the corpse is. To right the wasted wrong that Ricky started. To course correct the mistakes of the sacrifice. To finish what Ricky couldn't handle.

"We can't go back there," Kit warns me on the phone.

I had suggested that we all go back to the Aztakea Woods, to the spot where Gary was killed, to do our own ritual. The five of us had said we were going to start our own circle and everything, right? And now with the death of their leader, the Knights of the Black Circle were pretty much defunct, and it would be our time to be the new circle in town! I tried to word it gently, playfully, but the need to go there, to open the portal is strong and full of fire inside me. But Kit, thank the world for beautiful and level-headed Kit, is once again the voice of reason. She is one hundred percent right when she says we can't go there. There is still police tape around the area, and the investigation is still on-going because of the two other boys who were allegedly involved. "It's too risky," she says with her sweet, squeaky, baby-doll voice, and I can't help but smile to myself when she says it.

"Of all the risky things we've done together?" I goad. "Don't ya wanna have like, the ultimate high? The ultimate adventure? C'mon! It'll be like our last hurrah. One last fucked-up journey before we have to grow up and shit, or something corny like that!"

"Well, duh!" she squeals. "You know I'm all for it! You know I'm your right-hand chick! But Joeph, this is, like, fucked-up shit. Those boys were arrested. They killed poor Gary. Ricky is dead. We might wanna sit this one out and kinda stay far from any police stuff."

I scream at her on the inside. "Fine, fine, fine," I relent, trying to think of another way, another place.

I think back to all the other times I've glimpsed the glorious tear in the sky, the celestial smile splitting the universe wide open. The Amityville Horror House—not an ideal location to do a Satanic ritual (stupid, Ricky; you were too drugged up to figure that one out), and the first night I hooked up with Seth ... and at that very moment Kit and I simultaneously say, "The sump."

And it all makes sense. Everything is right with the world.

Kit meets me at the corner of Pickett and Sutton and we cheerily walk over to the sump. The others are already there by the time we get to our spot—Seth, Dan, Thomas, and *Carmen?* I nudge Kit's arm hard with my elbow when I see her in the distance.

"Ow! What the fuck, Joeph!" she squeals, rubbing herself.

"What do you mean, what the fuck? Do you see what I see or not? What the fuck is she doing here?"

"I guess they got back together. You know that's their way. Why? Are you jealous or something?"

I pull her arm, forcing her to stop in her tracks, and swivel her around to face me. "Are you serious? I could give a shit less. It's just..."

"I know," she says quietly with a smile. "I kinda hate her too."

I smile back and throw my arm around her shoulder to let her know it's okay. But it's not okay. My blood boils.

Thomas takes a guzzle from his beer bottle. "Well, well, well!" he bellows as we come into full view. "Look what the cat dragged in!"

"Har har," I say dryly. I drop my black knapsack onto the ground next to a silver boom box and walk over to Seth to give him a big sloppy kiss.

"Hey, you!" Seth smiles brightly, and I can feel Thomas squirm with rage and jealousy.

"Ohhh," Kit sings as she flocks to Dan's side. "This is a proper party, isn't it?" She grabs his beer and takes a swig.

I grab Seth's hands and drag him to the grass. "Ahhh, you brought it!" I say, motioning to the radio.

"Just like you asked."

"Well, turn that shit up!"

He smiles wide at me again. "Yes, ma'am!" He leans over and cranks up the volume to some Black Sabbath song, and Dan howls in excitement.

Everyone else gathers around me and Seth and sits down in a circle. The six of us. The three couples—Seth and me, Kit and Dan, Carmen and Thomas—all sit next to each other, closing the circle as the unlikely coven.

But the balance is off.

My head starts to throb again above my eyes. The sensation makes me wince a little and Seth mumbles, "You okay?" at my movement.

"Yeah, yeah, fine," I mumble back so that no one else but him can hear.

"Soooo, this is it!" Dan declares. "This is like, the end of an era and shit."

Thomas pulls Carmen into the crook of his arm. "Yeah, guess we're gonna have to like, get jobs and whatnot. And do stuff."

Dan twists his face at him and the two blurt out, "Nahhhh," simultaneously, laugh, and high-five each other.

"Hey, Seth, man, you got that Trent weed or what?" Dan blurts out after his laughing spell.

"Trent weed?" Carmen questions before sipping her drink. It's some purple, wine-cooler shit drink that's all the rage these days. "What's that?"

"Yo! Dude! Shut the fuck up with that! I fucking swore you to secrecy!" Seth yells.

"Please!" Dan huffs. "We're done with youth. Who gives a shit who knows? Not like it matters or anything."

"It was only just the best, most intense bud you've ever had," Kit says to Carmen in a taunting way. Like, nah, nah, nah, you didn't have some. Kit looks at me and gives me a mean-girl nod and my heart overflows with her loyalty.

"Oh," Carmen says, the bite in her voice trying to strike us down. "So, Seth, you got any? I'd love to try it." Thomas looks at her sharply. It's obvious he's annoyed.

"Hmmmm..." I say, my voice trailing. "I think I have something a little bit better." I reach behind me, dig into my knapsack, and pull out a paper plate covered in tinfoil. I pull back the foil to reveal a plateful of my mother's most delicious cookies.

A family recipe.

Kit squeals in delight. "Oh my God, Joephie! Is that what I think they are?"

"Your mom's cookies?" Seth adds.

"Oh yes. But I gave them a little something special." I wink at them. Like how a normal person sharing a secret with their friends would do.

Kit leans over and plants a giant smacking kiss on my cheek. "Holy shit! Have I ever told you that you are like the bestest friend in the world?"

"Only about a thousand times!" I gush and hand her the plate. She grabs a cookie, gingerly nibbles the edge, and passes the plate to Dan who then passes it around the rest of the circle.

Seth holds his up in front of him, like a dark priest holding up an oversized Eucharist in front of his congregation. "To us," he declares.

We all follow suit, repeat the words, and take the first big ceremonious bite of our cookies.

"Should we have our own name or something?" Dan asks through a mouthful of cookie.

"No way!" Kit says punching him in the arm. "We don't need a name. We're just... Us!" She smiles, proud of herself, proud of her assertion.

It happens almost instantly—the tingling, the wave. I feel as though the second the special dessert hit the back of my throat, I start to feel it. Faster than Trent's weed. Stronger than Trent's weed. I balance myself on my arms behind me and gaze up at the sky searching for a sign of my portal. It's the perfect summer night—clear sky, every star visible, the full moon shining down on Us in our circle of six, a breeze gently blowing across the indentation of the sumpland, the song of the woods singing to me. I breathe in the fresh air to clear my mind to hear the song better, and I remember the cassette from Trent! I reach back into my bag and toss it to Seth. "Play this," I say, but my voice feels kinda wobbly. He takes it and puts it in the boom box. "Turn it up," I command, and he listens to me, the twisted song beginning to fill the sumpland.

"This is weird!" Carmen says, her nose kinda turning up in disgust. "What is this?"

"I don't know," I reply. "Trent gave it to me. I think it's kinda pretty."

I know my answer doesn't satisfy her, though. I know the music splits in her head, carving out all the little pink areas, making her feel lost and confused and dazed and drugged and helpless. It's written on her face in big bold ancient carvings, and in the center of her forehead an X appears in tiny mini flames. I blink my eyes to rid myself of the vision as Kit puts her hand on my knee and looks dreamily at me, intoxication melting all over her face and glazing over her eyes. "You're kinda pretty."

My head wobbles in her direction. "Kinda?" I tease.

She runs her hand up my thigh and pulls my leg to the ground. "No. Totally. Like, a fox. Total fox," she slurs.

"Total," Thomas repeats, but I don't think he meant to say that out loud. His mouth clamps with a pop as soon as the word leaves his lips, and Carmen stands up in a huff.

"Total? Total? Really, Tommy?"

He reaches his arm up to grab her wrist, but in his inebriation, it's the most feeble grab attempt I've ever seen! She jerks away from him, with full-body force that nearly drops her back to the ground. She stumbles over her own feet and corrects her stance. We all jump up at once. I don't know why; it just kinda happens.

"I... um... I think I gotta go, Tommy," she stammers.

"Wait, Car, don't!" he protests. "You're so fucked up. You can't get home."

She looks at all of us and confusion darkens her brown eyes. The moonlight casts shadows on her face, giving her a weird, demonic look.

You're fine. You'll be okay.

"No, no, no. I'm fine. I'll be okay. I can walk. I need to walk this off."

You don't belong here.

"I don't belong here," she mutters, her voice struggling to prevent the words, but they manage to come out. She turns on her heels and stumbles into the darkness.

Thomas makes a move to stop her, but Seth grabs his shoulder. "Let her go, man. Let her go. Don't let her ruin your buzz."

Thomas puts his head into his hands and wails. "This is fucking bullshit! What the fuck? Why the fuck is she so weird! And Ricky's dead! He's dead! Why did he kill himself, man? Why!"

He unleashes all his emotions into his palms. His drunken, drug-induced outburst is nauseating.

Stop it, Thomas. Just stop.

Suddenly, he quiets himself, looks up from his hands, and starts laughing insanely.

"Aww yeah… there's our boy!" Dan cheers, and everyone starts to clap.

The song on the tape changes, but does it? I can't really tell if there are actual tracks of songs or if it's one continuous song. Does it even matter? Whatever it is, it stirs me. Wakens me. Focuses me. I look up to the sky, and amidst the stars, the moon, the treetops, and the cloudless dome, I see *it* spark into existence. *The portal.* It hovers like a little sparkler on the Fourth of July, fizzing and sputtering, trying to gain traction to open up and swallow the world.

I turn my attention back to Kit. "Still a fox?"

She turns her back on Dan and takes a step forward to face me. "Oh yeah, such a fox."

I extend my arm and sweep her blonde bangs from her face. Her glossy lips shimmer in the moonlight. Are they cherry tonight? Bubblegum? Only one way to find out, I suppose, so I tilt my head and pull her into a deep kiss.

Raspberry. Tart and sweet. I should have known.

"Wait! What?" Thomas exclaims, and the boys all kinda hoot and holler at Kit and me making out.

Seth comes up behind me and pulls my hair to the side. He runs his fingers down the side of my neck and tugs my shirt to the side of my shoulder. Swiftly, he pulls one arm through the neck hole and slides the other side down my body. Thomas kneels in between me and Kit, and he lifts each of my legs, removes my shirt from my ankles and tosses it aside by the boom box. His hands reach up, and in an instant he unhooks the button of my jean shorts and slides them down along with my panties. I assume he does the same to Kit.

Seth unhooks the latch of my bra, glides the straps off the front of me, and tosses it into the pile of clothes. 'Cause there's a pile of clothes. All of ours. Seth presses himself against me. Seth gropes my breasts, tugging at my nipples, making my hips dance from the pleasure. The skin of his upper body has a thin layer of sweat coating it. In my head, I turn around to lick his chest—to taste the salty shimmer of his body, but I'm too enraptured with Kit's kiss to pull away. It's slow and gentle, then passionate and hard. I want to eat her raspberry lips and feel the flesh slide down my throat.

My eyes flutter open for a second to see Dan behind Kit kissing her neck, fondling her breasts in the same way Seth does to me. They knead our flesh and grind their hardened bodies against our backsides in perfect rhythm, in perfect time to the hypnotic music. Thomas, still kneeling in the center of this upright circle of flesh, extends his arms and slides each of his hands on the inner part of Kit and my thighs. At the same time, he enters two fingers inside of us. I know this because Kit and I both kinda jolt from the sensation simultaneously. Kit gives a soft squeak as

Thomas presses on us. Up and down. Up and down. Moving in and out of our bodies. But we continue to kiss—holding each other's forearms, our tongues dancing wildly to the song. Seth and Dan on us, Thomas's fingers inside us.

Seth continues his assault on my chest. His fingernails dig into my pale skin, leaving me with raw and red track marks up and down my sides and underneath the soft spots of my breasts. His hard organ is nestled between the flesh of my backside rocking up and down but never going inside, but I sense his forcefulness could be from anger. Or is it jealousy? Does he not like how I moan from Thomas's touch? Because I moan. Oh, yes! I moan! Thomas drives three fingers now to the hilt of his digits, and my body starts to rise, starts to swell. My stomach quivers, and it's hard to stand completely upright. Kit grabs my cheeks eagerly, and with each of Thomas's thrusts, she increases the ferocity of her kiss. Her teeth scrape against my lips. We nip at each other's tongues as if we were seeking to draw blood. With one last plunge, my insides explode all over his fingers.

"Holy shit!" he exclaims. He exits Kit and me, spreads my legs a little farther apart, and buries his face in my crevice. His tongue tries desperately to dart in and out of me, trying to lap up any last remains of my excitement.

With Thomas no longer connected to Kit, Dan clutches her hard against his chest, drops her to her knees in the grass, and bends her over, mounting her like a lion does when mating with his lioness. But they *are* lions in the moonlight. I envision their golden shapes of glittering bodies flashing in and out of my mind's eye. He claws at her back and says something vile out loud. I don't know what it is because I can't hear very well above the music, the pulse of the moon, the song of the woods, and the blood rushing inside my ears with pleasure, but whatever it is, Kit's face darkens, and terror enters her eyes as she looks up at me with her pretty little lioness face. "No, wait!" she cries out to him in a split-second moment of clarity, but he drives himself inside of her, and she howls into the night sky.

The night sky.

I hadn't been paying attention, but when I look up right above where Kit and Dan do unspeakable things, I see it is there. It's formed! And it's huge! A pulsing light shimmering like their wild animal bodies, and the tear in the center growing, growing, growing. This is it. I know I will see the other side of that portal tonight. *Whatever the cost.*

Thomas ends his uneventful tongue lashing of my sex and stands up in front of me. He grabs my face and kisses me furiously—the taste of his mouth mixed with the warm honey of me. His tongue is rough and darts in and out of my mouth like a thin baby snake. It's hard to keep a rhythm with his awkward kiss, and for a second, I think: *Has he ever kissed a girl before?* I think Thomas senses my displeasure, and in a panic, he kisses me faster and harder, and grinds his penis on the inside of my thigh. He slides back and forth on the remnants of wetness, trying to poke at my opening, hoping to drive himself in.

Seth's organ taps against the inside of my other thigh, dangerously close to me as well. The two cocks fight for dominance of my domain—fighting for a lordship in my castle. Each of their organs teases me, brushes against my nether lips, dancing with each other in what feels like a delicate war for authority over me. Lightning flashes from cloud to cloud—the built-up electricity releasing itself in the summer sky. It startles Thomas, and for a moment, he stops kissing me and looks up. This gives Seth the opportunity to pivot my shoulders around to face him and only him. Thomas realizes he has lost the alpha position and, with cock in hand, slinks over to the bodies of Kit and Dan who are finishing their own dance. Dan's grunting echoes in the night to signal he's finished his violation of Kit.

As soon as we're face to face, Seth runs his arms protectively up my back and kisses up and down my neck and nibbles on my earlobe. "Do you remember what I told you that night we were together in the sump?" he whispers.

"That you so very badly wanted to fuck me?" I answer coyly.

"Uh huh," he says between bites.

I swoon from the goosebumps blooming on my body. "And now?" I ask.

He pulls back and stares me deep in the eyes. They are like the ocean. Blue-green waves crash over the moonlit sand, inviting me into their deepest, darkest depths. I glance at the sky and the portal has expanded its position amongst the stars.

The stars have shifted.

And the music fills the sump. Fills my head. Makes me sway back and forth as Seth gently pulls me down to the grass. I hesitate a little and say, "Kit." Seth looks to the right of us, to where Kit lies naked in the grass with her legs spread open. The small tuft of blonde hair from her sex glistens in the pulsating light of the portal. Somehow, I feel like I'm the only one who sees it though. Thomas lies beside her, petting the insides of her thighs and stroking the upper part of her body gently. Seth understands exactly what I mean and pulls our bodies closer to her. She smiles dreamily at me—a closed-mouth, squinty-eyed smile.

She extends her arm and wiggles her fingers signaling for me to grab her hand. "Joephie," she sings, and her baby-doll voice is like a symphony in my head. "You taste like maple syrup."

"Yeah, she does," Thomas mumbles, but I don't think anyone else heard him.

"You taste like raspberries," I say.

"Raspberries covered in maple syrup," Kit moans.

Thomas shimmies his body in between her legs, and she squeezes my hand tight when he enters her.

Seth starts at my ankles and slowly kisses his way up. He stops briefly at my warm crevice, burrowing his head for a second to lap at me with three quick licks. He rises and continues upward, kissing my stomach, licking the track marks he made with his short nails. Finally, he reaches my neck. He whispers something in my ear, but I can't make out the words because my head is filled with the music, the song of the woods, the growing electric pulse of the portal that widens in the sky, and Kit's ecstatic screams of pleasure from Thomas's thrusts.

And then it happens.

Seth plunges himself inside me, and my hips writhe at the sensation of it all. Lightning flashes among the clouds again, but I'm not sure if it actually happened in the sky or in my head because there are still shimmery flashes behind my eyes. I squeeze hard on Kit's hand and cry out—in both pleasure and pain because my insides widen and swell, yet they clamp down on Seth's cock driving him wild and heightening his thrusts. I feel him all over me—every inch, every ridge, every slick patch of flesh on, in, around, hovering, moving, throbbing. Seth pushes and grinds into me and we fall into a rhythm that syncopates with the motions of Thomas and Kit. We are the perfect circle of bodies and connectivity. Seth inside of me, Thomas inside of Kit, Kit and I joined together in clasped hands completing the chain. Kit and I turn our heads to face each other. We lock eyes and in my mind, I send images to her of us kissing again. I know she receives them because she bites her bottom lip the way I did to her before. We're completely connected—holding hands, staring longingly at each other, feeling the jamming organs of our lovers at the exact same time. We're together. She's with me.

After a few moments, I look away from Kit and peek over Seth's sweaty shoulder and up into that full moon night sky, and with every stab from him, the mouth of the portal opens wider and wider. Every time I feel my insides climb higher to crescendo, the lights surrounding the tear pulse brighter and brighter.

A voice moans. Not Kit or Thomas, and not me or Seth. Another voice.

Dan's voice.

Naked, Dan kneels in the grass between the two body sets of fornication. He rocks back and forth, eyes closed, swaying with the music. He outstretches his arms, revealing dark red circles carved into the flesh of his forearms. The blood drips down in long lines, snaking in the grooves of his palms and rolling off his fingertips into the grass.

He is the fifth point of the star. The fifth point of the circle.

The portal expands.

My body rises with the sensation of levitation. The energy grows and flows, and I know it's powerful enough to lift both me and Seth into the portal to take us far away. Consume me. Consume us.

Kit grips me tighter and quicker. Her hand thrusts mirror Thomas's cock plummeting into her and the pulsating opening of the tear in the sky. I pump my hand back to let her know I feel it, too. 'Cause I feel it all. I feel Thomas inside of me, fighting for space with Seth. I feel Kit's insides hungrily accepting and absorbing Thomas and Seth's throbbing organs. I feel Dan's life force spilling into the Earth. And I feel that at any moment, my body will disintegrate to nothing and be swept up into the oblivion of the beyond.

And Hell will be unleashed.

My body tenses as I hear that voice in my head. Trent's voice, but not Trent's voice. The demon Trent. The demon.

"Joephie," Kit moans. "There's something wrong with Dan."

I ignore her and focus on Seth.

"Joephie," she says louder. "Look at Dan. He's not right."

I look at Dan. He's encompassed in red light and white foam bubbles around his mouth.

"Oh, God!" Kit screams. "Someone help Dan! Help him!" She releases my hand. The tear in the sky starts to shrink up. In a panic, I push Seth off. His penis slithers out of me, but it's not a cock, it's a long green snake with red eyes and fangs that hang over its mouth. Quickly, I scramble on my knees to inspect Dan.

He's not dead yet.

Not dead yet.

Not dead yet.

Kit screams. Thomas and Seth frantically yell, "Joephie!?"

"Jesus Christ, stop!"

150

Or something like that.

Not dead yet.

I grip my hands around his throat and squeeze. The portal struggles to maintain its wide opening, but I know it's diminishing. I need to stop it.

Not dead yet.

"Please! Joephie! Stop!"

Not dead yet.

Squeezing tighter.

Rip in the sky withering.

"Joephie! What are you doing!?"

I think it's Thomas who comes up behind me and strikes me in the back of the head.

Everything goes black.

Not dead yet.

Chapter 11

Sunday, March 6th 1966
The Turner Residence
91 Beth Avenue
Franklin Square, New York
Night Before the Full Moon

The ad in the classified section of the newspaper read: *"Babysitter Wanted: Mornings Only. 5 days a week, school days, $25 a week flat. Call for interview."* It was so small; it was a wonder how anyone would even see it buried in the sea of other "wanteds." Nancy Turner took her red pen and gave it a circle. It seemed easy enough, and the per-week pay was enticing. Besides, there weren't very many other red circles on the page, and circling any prospective opportunity was better than nothing. There wasn't much work available for six-months pregnant women.

Nancy lived in a one-bedroom basement apartment with her post office worker husband Brian. For just the two of them, their lifestyle was pretty simple and quaint—had been since they had gotten married four years ago. Nancy enjoyed a life as a stay-at-home wife, and Brian worked the streets delivering mail to his happy-town neighbors. It wasn't lavish or luxurious, but they got by. But now, with an increase in monthly bills—doctor's visits, new furniture, another mouth to feed, and a place with at least a second bedroom—the pressure on Brian to provide was a heavy weight. Nancy had often brought up the idea of buying a house, but Brian wasn't convinced that was the right way to go. He was worried about inflation rising because of the Vietnam War. He was worried about being drafted as there were continuous rumors about the draft lottery coming back. So to help out, Nancy did odd jobs—cleaning lady, a short stint in retail—she even cut the neighbors' hair. As her belly grew, her career opportunities shrank.

When Brian rubbed his eyes and stumbled into the kitchen for breakfast, she said, "It'd just be for three months. Just until school is over and the baby is born. What harm could it bring, right? It'd be easy money. Do you think I should do it?"

He yawned and huffed and hawed. "Sounds easy enough, I guess."

"A few hundred extra dollars? Why not?"

"Sure, why not?" he relented.

"So, you think I should call today for the interview?"

"Well, Jesus Christ, Nance! What do you think? If you don't call today, someone else will!"

Yes, he was right. Of course, he was right. He was always right.

Nancy hesitantly called the number in the ad after breakfast. She didn't know why, but her fingers slipped a few times in the rotary holes on the phone. She chalked it up to her nerves and took a few deep breaths when the line rang on the other end. "It's just a job. Just a babysitting job," she whispered to herself as a mantra to calm down. But the line rang and rang, and nobody picked up, and a twinge of failure crept up into her chest. *Maybe they don't want me? Maybe I'm not good enough? Maybe I'm not worthy?* she thought. "Oh, stop being ridiculous, Nance!" she said out loud at the exact moment a female voice answered "Hello?"

Taken off guard, poor Nancy, now wondering if the voice on the other end heard what she had said, stuttered, "Um... hi... hello... I... um... my name is Nancy. Nancy Turner. I'm calling about the ad in the paper this morning. For the babysitting position?"

Nancy could hear the woman take a deep breath and exhale with a sigh of relief. "Hello, Nancy!" she boomed, and Nancy could practically see the woman's smile through the phone line. "I'm so glad you called. My name is Barbara. Barbara Thorne. Our situation is a little bit... unconventional, you could say."

"Unconventional? How so?"

"Well," Barbara sighed, "I just need childcare for my two kids in the mornings. I need someone here before school—to get them ready, feed them breakfast, double check that their homework has been done the night before, stuff like that. Ya know, the little incidentals. My husband and I will be here at the apartment with you, but we'll be getting ourselves ready for the day, and we can't give the children the attention they need. Then, we'll need you to walk them to school, which is right down the block from our apartment."

"Oh," Nancy said. "What about pick-up in the afternoon?"

"No, no, no. My husband or I will be able to get them from school. It's strictly a morning gig. School starts at 8:30 a.m., so I was thinking start time would be 7:00 a.m."

"Oh," Nancy repeated.

"Twenty-five dollars a week, whether the kids have school or not. There are a few days that are vacation days, so you'll get a little break." Barbara gave a little laugh. Her voice was like dark, rich honey—smooth, but slow moving. Sweet, but distinct. "Once school is over in June, the job will end."

"I'm pregnant," Nancy blurted. She closed her eyes waiting for the response of "oh, that's not going to work for us, sorry" because she had heard it a few other times in her odd-job hunt. The pause on the other end sent Nancy into a tailspin of anxiety, and she thought about just hanging up the line right then and there.

"Wow! When are you due?" Barbara gushed like an old friend hearing this wonderful news for the first time, and Nancy slowly opened her eyes in shock. She hadn't expected such a jubilant response.

"June. June 6th. But you know how those dates are."

"That's fantastic! Is this your first?"

"Mmm hmmm."

"Super! That's absolutely super!"

Nancy's nerves quelled, and she smiled to herself.

"So..." Barbara began, "can you start on Monday?"

"Monday? As in, tomorrow Monday?"

"Oh my Lord! It's Sunday, isn't it? Jeez Louise! Yes. Tomorrow. Please say you can start tomorrow?"

"But don't you want to meet me for an interview?"

"Oh no! This was interview enough. What do you say? Can you do it?"

"Um... yeah. Sure," Nancy stammered with uncertainty.

"Great!" Barbara exclaimed. "Grab a pen and paper, and I'll give you the address."

Monday, March 7th 1966
The Thorne Residence
76 Rose Avenue
Franklin Square, New York
Morning of the Full Moon

Nancy ran her sweaty hands down the sides of her tawny pea coat. The force of the morning air whipped her brown hair to the side and sent a chill on her bare neck. *Should have worn a scarf,* she thought. Outside the Thorne residence, she anticipated what would happen when she finally rang the bell. Would they be nice? Would they like her? Would she like the children? Is she even up for doing this? Trying to steady her nerves, she inhaled deeply and exhaled with a smoky gust. Her watch read 6:50 a.m. Ten minutes early, but she wanted to make a good first impression.

"Now or never!" she said and rang the bell.

Within moments, someone bounded on the steps, and the wooden door flung open from the inside leaving the screen door barrier between them. "Nancy?" the woman on the other side asked?

"Barbara?" Nancy replied.

The woman smiled wide and opened the secondary door. "Come on in! It's cold this morning!"

She's stunning! Nancy thought upon seeing Barbara's face in full view. Everything about her visage was pure perfection—her black eyes were like two pieces of shimmering onyx set against her pale, alabaster white skin. Like porcelain. Like a China doll with ruby red lips. Her high cheekbones jutted out with a sharp angle, almost giving her a villainous look like Maleficent from the movie *Sleeping Beauty*, but not at all cartoonish or evil.

Nancy climbed the last step of the front staircase and went into the house. "Yeah. Sorry I'm a little early."

Barbara raised one of her perfectly arched eyebrows. "Don't be silly! Glad you did. Welcome!" She extended her hand and shook Nancy's vigorously before turning on her heels and heading up the long stairway to the second story apartment. Her long, dark hair swished over her shoulders and hung heavy down her back. Heavy black hair with strands of silver racing like lightning across the night sky. Barbara was too young to have gray hair like that, and Nancy thought: *Wow, Lily Munster in the flesh!*

With every step, Barbara's black velvet dress dragged behind her. Nancy followed closely and observed everything about the home. The stairwell was long and narrow, and strangely dark, like a tunnel rising from the darkest depths of an ancient cavern. The wooden steps creaked with each footfall, creating an eerie squeaking sound in the confined space. "Just be careful on the dark mornings 'cause there isn't a light and this stairwell is kinda tricky," Barbara said, as if reading Nancy's mind.

"Oh, yeah, no sweat."

Barbara opened the door at the top of the steps and moved to the side so Nancy could squeeze in. "The kids are just getting up. I'll walk you through the routine and familiarize you with the apartment and such."

"Sounds good."

"Here, let me take your coat."

"Oh yeah, yeah," Nancy stammered, removing her garment and passing it to Barbara.

Barbara opened a closet door in the foyer and hung it up. "Oh look! Look at your belly! Such a beautiful thing!" she gushed.

Instinctively, Nancy placed both hands on top of her tummy bulge and smiled. "Not so beautiful when it squirms around when I'm trying to sleep."

Both women chuckled at the exchange of womanhood pleasantries. Then, Barbara clasped her hands together and said, "Okay. House tour!" and led Nancy throughout the two-bedroom, one-bathroom apartment, pointing out all the important and necessary things that she might need or need to get to in the mornings while taking care of the children. It all flowed so simply and so normally, like an average American working family. Much like what Nancy had hoped she and Brian would be like one day.

However, things didn't seem to add up on this tour. As a matter of fact, things seemed a little too perfect, like how on first glance everything in the home had a place, was in its place, and belonged in its place. Neat. Packaged. *Dream-like*. Barbara spoke quickly and smoothly, giving all the technical instructions a mother would give to the new babysitter. "Here's the phone. All the emergency contact numbers are here if ever there's a time when Galen and I leave before you guys do. The kids love pancakes in the morning. They need to be told to brush their teeth." The refrigerator displayed handprint paintings with smiley faces done by the children and a piece of torn notebook paper that read "Sisterhood Meeting, 8:00 p.m."

Barbara moved about the apartment as if she were gliding through air—swiftly, gracefully—pointing out points of interest in the home with almost magical flicks of her wrist. It all seemed so wonderful and picture-perfect, but every now and then, Nancy caught a flicker from the corner of her eye, like something shifting in the air, like a ripple, or static coming through the television. And when she would pause and inspect certain things within the home, she squinted her eyes as if to see beyond a layer of haze, a layer of fairy dust concealing the truth. Hanging in the living room was a painting of a lion in a circus, but when Nancy squinted hard enough, she saw it was actually a painting of a lion with its mouth gaping open and a person, headfirst inside. Blood dripped from the sides of the lion's mouth and onto a five-pointed circle on the floor. Nancy blinked hard, trying to erase the image from her mind.

"You okay?" Barbara said, pausing the house tour.

"Oh yes. I'm fine," Nancy lied.

The den was dimly lit with soft candelabra lightbulbs, the type that flicker to give the appearance of actual flames in the candle holder. "The kids leave their school stuff in here every night," Barbara said pointing to the desk in the center of the room. Nancy noticed the bookshelves along the sides of the walls had tons of books on them — old books, ancient books, books with titles like *Malleus Maleficarum*, *An Encyclopedia of Witches*, *Demoniality*, *Letters on Demonology and Witchcraft*, and *Blodheksa, Blodbrødre, og Blodsøster*. But she couldn't be sure if that's what she actually saw. It probably wasn't real. Neither were the stone statues in the hallway leading down to the children's bedroom, right? The demon bust with horns mounted on a black lacquered pedestal or the headless naked woman with a snake wrapped around her body.

"And this is Gretchen and David's room," Barbara said, guiding Nancy to the children's dwelling. "Gretchen is five, David is seven. We hate that we have to make them share a room right now, but they're still young enough for it to not be weird. We plan on moving to a bigger place anyway, and hopefully, add a third to our little coven."

Nancy widened her eyes at Barbara's peculiar choice of words. She craned her neck into the children's room to see the two little ones perfectly perched on their respective bunk beds. They both smiled at her and gave little childlike waves.

"Hi!" Nancy said cheerfully.

"Kids this is Nancy. She's going to be taking care of you guys in the mornings and walking you to school."

"Hi, Nancy," the children said simultaneously. Their pale white faces were framed with shaggy black hair, and their eerie smiles made Nancy uneasy for a split second, but she was put at comfortable ease when little Gretchen squealed with a giggle, "Nancy, our Nanny!"

Friday, March 25th 1966
The Thorne Residence
76 Rose Avenue
Franklin Square, New York
Night of the Waxing Crescent Moon

The pay was good, and the gig was easy. Pancakes, eggs, or cereal were the common breakfast choices for the kids. Homework was never a problem, as Gretchen was only in kindergarten and had none, and David usually had the most basic of second grade tasks to complete. They were sweet and loving and took to her right away, and Nancy genuinely loved them back. Sometimes David sassed when he was told to brush his teeth, but nothing outside of the typical little boy attitude. Their walks to school were always the best—they had super silly conversations and Nancy felt like she was truly connecting with their kid brains. It was excellent preparation for the arrival of her own.

By the end of the first week, though, there were two mornings where Barbara and her husband were not at home (come to think of it, Nancy had never actually met Mr. Thorne). There was a note on the fridge saying, "Hey Nancy, left at 7:10 a.m. for an emergency meeting. Sorry. They were still sleeping," and it was posted right next to a new paper that read "Brotherhood Meeting 7:00 p.m." By the second week, Barbara had asked if Nancy could pick the kids up from school at 3:00 p.m. and sit with them until she or her husband got home from work. "Oh please, Nance? I'm in such a bind at the office," Barbara had said. And really, even though it wasn't part of the original agreement, it was not a big deal because Nancy wasn't doing anything *anyway*, and she really truly loved being around those kids. "She's taking advantage of you! Extra work and no extra pay!" Nancy's husband Brian had barked. But Nancy ignored him and his ignorant remarks. She didn't see it that way. She saw it as helping out a friend in need and helping the kids she had become so attached to.

That morning, Barbara had asked Nancy to pick up the kids again from school, to which Nancy gleefully said yes. On the walk over to school, Gretchen clutched Nancy's hand and swung them both back and forth like she usually did. "What kind of baby are you having?" Gretchen asked.

Nancy smiled. "What do you mean, sweetie?"

"A boy or a girl?"

"Oh, I don't know. I won't know until the baby is born."

"Hmmm... what do you want to have?"

"It doesn't matter to me," Nancy beamed. "As long as it's happy and healthy."

"Well, it's definitely healthy," David mumbled ominously.

Nancy couldn't be sure if she had heard him correctly, so she asked him to repeat. "What was that, David?"

"Nothing. Never mind."

Gretchen yanked on Nancy's arm, stopping them in their tracks. She took off one of her little black mittens, slid her bare hand underneath Nancy's coat and pressed against her stomach.

"Gretchen! Not so hard!" she protested and pulled back a little, but the baby wiggled inside of her, almost in synch with the little girl's hands.

Gretchen's face lit up when the baby jolted and kicked.

"Wow!" Nancy said in a sing-songy tone. "Did you feel the baby kick at you? It must really like you!"

Gretchen stayed there, feeling the baby squirm a few more moments. Then, she removed her hand and put her mitten back on. "It's a girl," she declared. "She told me so."

Nancy raised her eyebrows. "Oooohh… she did, did she?"

"Yep! She has such a pretty name, too."

"Hmmmm… like *Gretchen*?" Nancy teased and bent down to tickle the girl.

Gretchen giggled. "No. Gretchen is her middle name."

"So what's her first name?" Nancy teased playfully.

"Josephine. She told me that too. Princess Joephie Gretchen Bluebell Thorne."

Nancy couldn't help but laugh at the little girl's innocence. What a darling name for a darling baby. "Sure, sweetie. Sounds good to me."

Nancy didn't feel so well after dropping the kids off at school. A searing pain shot down her legs, and she just attributed it to the baby pressing on her sciatic nerve. By the time she got home, though, she started to feel hot. Afraid she was coming down with something, she decided to head it off at the pass and jump in the shower to cool down. When she removed her clothing and looked at herself in the mirror, she noticed a long red mark across the circumference of her stomach, like a ligature mark of someone having been strangled. Scared that something might be wrong with the baby, she called her doctor, and he said to come in right away to be on the safe side. She called Brian at work to let him know what was going on, then she called Barbara's work number to tell her she wouldn't be able to pick up the kids, but Barbara wasn't there, and she left a message with her co-worker. Just for double insurance, Nancy decided to let the kids' school know of the situation.

"Hi, my name is Nancy Turner," she said frantically to the receptionist. "I'm the babysitter for David and Gretchen Thorne. I was supposed to pick them up from school today, but I'm having a medical issue and need to get to my doctor right away. I'm not sure how long I will be. I called their mother at work but had to leave a message with a co-worker."

"Ma'am?" the receptionist questioned. "Who did you say you were again?"

"Nancy. Nancy Turner. I'm supposed to pick up the Thorne children, but I have an emergency, and I can't get ahold of their mother, so could you please…"

"Okay. Not a problem. We'll reach the parent. What were the children's names again?"

"Thorne. David in the second grade, and Gretchen in kindergarten."

"Ms. Turner, are you sure you called the right school?"

"What? What are you talking about? Of course, I called the right school! Please, just try to reach their mother, Barbara Thorne."

"Ma'am, I'm really not sure what to tell you, but there are no Thorne children who attend Polk Street Elementary. There's no David or Gretchen Thorne here."

A sharp pain in her stomach doubled Nancy over, causing her to drop the phone. She let out a shrill cry of agony as the baby twisted and turned in the womb with ferocious kicks and jolts. She fell to the floor, arm outstretched with the phone receiver in her hand. Her eyes shifted in and out of focus, as if she were going in and out of consciousness. In the corner of the room, she could have sworn she saw a light—a dancing, brilliant light, moving and opening, and widening like a mouth with starry teeth coming for her. "It's going to eat me!" she screamed. "It's going to eat me and take my baby!" The baby tumbled and somersaulted, making Nancy sick with its relentless movements. Her head ached, and a paralyzing wave locked her in place on the floor with her eyes wide open and mouth agape, staring into the ripple, wondering when it would swallow her whole. She stayed like that until Brian came home from work.

Chapter 12

Thursday, February 10th 1994
The Shoreline Apartment Complex
1700 Neilson Way APT #1010
Santa Monica, California
Morning of the Night of the New Moon

A balmy breeze filters up from the Pacific Ocean and into the opened window of my 10th story apartment. It rouses me from yet another dreamless sleep, but I'm not really sleeping and I'm not really awake. I'm in that in-between state where my mind wants one thing, and my body wants another. I ask them both which they prefer, but I never get a straight answer, so I surrender to the now and here—the nowhere of the gaps of my mind and the uncertainty of my physiological desires.

Super deep, Joeph.

I want to huff out loud to myself, but I know once he realizes I'm awake, he'll want to bombard me with the usual battery of questions: "Did you dream last night?"

"Do you remember anything?"

"Did something get sparked in you?"

Blah, blah, blah. He always says that word — sparked. As if something one day is going to magically awaken in my brain and present to me some mystical answers to my never-ending questions about life and the universe. It's been almost ten years though. If nothing has come back to me by now, I doubt it ever will. So it's always the same. For the last three and a half years, the same mornings, the same questions, the same looks of longing, like he's trying to crack me open and find some hidden treasure.

I consciously keep my eyes closed when he tip-toes in from the en-suite bathroom and over to the bed. He lovingly pushes my hair away from my face, and I can feel his eyes staring at me. "Jo," he whispers. "Josie, you awake?"

I raise my eyebrows in acknowledgement.

"I'm going to work. I left your pills out for you on top of the dresser with some water."

"Mmm-hmm," I mumble into the pillow.

He kisses the top of my head. "Okay, see ya later. Love you."

"Mmm-mmm-mmm," I respond. My version of "love you, too."

He leaves, and I try hard to go back to sleep, but it's simply no use. I am compelled to get up and start the day. *Whatever that means.*

My mornings consist of taking my pills, coffee on the balcony of our 10th floor apartment, maybe a little TV, a shower perhaps, maybe catch a nap.

By mid-day I grab my drawing pad, sit back out on the balcony with another cup of coffee and maybe some lunch (like a sandwich or soup or a piece of fruit) and do some of my famous doodles. Afternoons are a crapshoot. I might go to the pool and swim some laps, maybe hit the gym, another round of meds, run some errands if I'm planning on making dinner, stroll the beach, go for a bike ride, or head up and down Santa Monica Boulevard with my artwork to make some money.

Of all the things that I thought I would be in this life, the last things were a "kept woman" and a "flash seller" — as in, I sell my drawings to tattoo parlors for their flash rotation. Like, people come into the shops, pick out a design on the wall or in a portfolio, and say "tattoo that on me" just like the fifty other people did before them. At first, the shop owners were ready and willing to kick me out, but when I told them who I was, that I'm Josephine Childes — *the* Josephine Childes — they changed their tunes real fast because a piece of artwork from a quasi-celebrity can fetch almost double the price of a regular flash piece.

I love Santa Monica — the ocean air, the laid-back vibe, all of it. It totally beats the hustle and bustle and gray, hazy days of New York. I'll admit it was kinda scary coming out here in August of '89 at 23 years old, all alone, and with just a few hundred dollars in my pocket. I thought I was eventually going to have to start tricking on Pico or something, but I was able to get a waitressing job right away, and one of my co-workers, Teri, said she could use another roommate, so I shacked-up at her place for a little bit. It was rough at first, eating Ramen packs and Poptarts to help save up some money, but Teri and I made it work. There were many electric-less nights because the bill wasn't paid, or a shower-less morning because the water was shut off, but we survived. I had managed to keep my past, or what I remembered from my past, a secret for some time, but in January of 1990, while pulling a double shift at the Sea Breeze Diner, I read an ad in the paper for a "psychiatric clinical trial" starting up at Santa Monica College and decided the pay was decent enough that I would give it a shot. Of course, that opened the floodgate of questions from Teri, and I eventually revealed to her my five-year stint in the South Oaks Psychiatric Ward on both involuntary and voluntary stay. After that bomb dropped, Teri and my relationship wasn't the same, to say the least.

The "psychiatric clinical trial" was run by young-buck doctor Javier "Javi" Efrain Peterson. He was conducting this whole shebang on lost memories and traumatic events splitting the human mind and blah, blah, blah. His goal was to be published in some prestigious medical journal and win some prestigious medical award. At 33 years old, he had already accomplished so much in his career, and when he approached the college with his proposal, they gave him a grant so large he didn't know what to do with it. This particular study was to be his life's work—the defining apex of his career, the one thing that would shape the rest of his life and practice, put him at the forefront of psychiatric medicine, and give him supreme credibility and clout in the field. He was smart, ambitious, dedicated to his work, and utterly adorable in that dorky way.

But I don't think he ever anticipated *me*.

I don't believe in love at first sight and all that lovey-dovey bullshit, but if I had to guess, he was attracted to me the first time I walked into the office. I actually think he fell in love with my story though, before he fell in love with me. I, on the other hand, took a little more convincing when he started to lay the charm on me. And I'll admit it, he's certainly not my type—the scholarly look— medium height, medium build, glasses and a stereotypical doctor mustache, polos and khakis. At first, I was more attracted to his brain and his willingness to "fix me" because, at the time, I really felt like I needed fixing. My attraction to his physical being kinda fell in place a little later on. I mean, I can't deny a good kisser!

Including me, Javi had five test cases—all women, all with some type of trauma and lost memories, but it was my situation that fascinated him most—a good, small-town drifter girl from New York with possible ties to an infamous Satanic cult has a psychotic break one night while hanging out with her friends (resulting in the death of one of them), spends five years in a psychiatric ward, fed a steady diet of anti-depressants, anti-anxieties, anti-psychotics, and has no recollection of the events surrounding or leading up to the incident. I was just what he was looking for. I was his perfect candidate, his perfect test subject. At first, he looked at me like a treasure map. The X was burned into me somewhere, and he just needed to uncover it. And he really did try so hard using hypnosis, talk sessions, music therapy, guided imagery, and even group sessions where he had all the patients of the trial come in to talk about their experiences. But nothing. My treasure was never found.

By June of 1990, our relationship had broken the patient-doctor boundaries, and Javi decided to abandon his research with his other patients, give up the study, call off the rest of the trials, and pay back whatever was owed on the grant so that we could be together. He had a small apartment on Santa Monica Boulevard at the time, so I left Teri and moved in with him. I stopped working at the Sea Breeze and hung out every day while he taught some classes at the college and saw some patients at the local clinic. He hated doing both. He always said that the students were stupid and only taking his class to fulfill their pre-requisites (because a psych class is apparently easier to take than a bio class) and that the people at the clinic were making up half the shit they told him in their sessions because they were looking to get prescription drugs.

But for me, it was kinda cool, ya know, being 24 years old, living right by the beach in Santa Monica (my dream), and having my older, doctor boyfriend supporting me. Yeah, who cared that when he came home at night, he sat me down and flung a thousand and one questions at me or tried to do some hypnosis sessions? I just figured he really cared about me and about helping me unlock my own personal secrets. He suggested going back to Long Island to do a "memory walk-about," but I was completely against that, and he supported my decision. Then, he introduced me to Automatic-Trance-Writing—a fairly new technique where the patient relaxes their mind and writes words or phrases freely without really thinking about it. Words and phrases never came to my mind. My trance-writing was image-based, and that's when I started my doodles.

Things with me and Javi were fine for about a year. He worked hard, I played hard, and we had some good times, but the apartment walls were closing in on us by the day, and his frustration at not advancing in his field fast enough was a constant black cloud looming over us. In June of 1991, my 25th birthday, he gave me a large box wrapped in silver glitter wrapping paper and topped with a gold bow. I knew he had whatever it was professionally wrapped because it was too perfectly done up. The box was a little bigger than the idea I had in my head. I mean, we'd briefly talked about getting married, but it wasn't like a forefront issue or anything. Maybe it was wishful thinking on my part, who knows?

His large brown eyes went wide with wonder when he plopped it in my lap and urged me to open it. So, I tore through the paper, the initial defeat of "oh, it's not an engagement ring" far from my mind. I sifted through the white tissue paper and pulled out a rudimentary bound book. It wasn't a store-bought book though; it was a manuscript with photocopied printed pages. I fanned through the pages before placing it back on my lap. The title page, what should have been the cover, read *Unlocking Josephine: A Case Study in Lost Memory Recovery by Dr. Javier Efrain Peterson*. Immediately, my face twisted, and I barked, "What the hell is this?"

"It's you! It's your story!" he beamed.

I folded my hands on top of the manuscript and very calmly said, "What in the holy fuck are you talking about?"

"I wrote this for you, about you. This is my work. The trial that took a life of its own. You had a story to tell, and now it will be told."

"Have you lost your fucking mind, Jav? First of all, why would you ever think I would want people to know about me..."

"I changed your name, Josie," he interrupted. "To protect you. I know how things work."

"Second of all, how the fuck does this end? You know I don't remember anything! We've tried for years to figure out what happened!"

He paused for a second and took a deep breath. "Well," he said hesitantly, "that part..."

Was a lie.

A big fat fucking lie.

In an attempt to make something real out of me, Javi completely fabricated the conclusion because he needed some kind of closure and end-game product. It burned him up when he couldn't get it for real, so he'd made it up. A perfect golden bow tied around the silver lie. And no one was fact checking the doctor extraordinaire, so who cared? A big-time publishing house gave Javi a big time advance, and the book was fast-tracked to hit the shelves in August. It didn't matter what I said or how I protested. It was a done deal.

To make up for it, to placate my anger and disgust at the situation, at the bottom of the box was a heart keychain with a shiny new key attached. The new key to our new luxury apartment at the Shoreline Apartment Complex—everything upgraded—10th floor, two-bedroom, ocean view, beach-front suite. The finest in all of Santa Monica. Rich blood. I shut my mouth real good after that, I mean, could I really argue with that proposition? And Javi, the psych doctor that he is, can be super convincing. Plus, he always knew how to make me feel safe, like I was his little bird with a broken wing that needed to be mended and cared for. He would never steer me in the wrong direction, right? I could always trust his guidance and wisdom. Because he was older, wiser, and had dragged me out of the goddamn gutter and saved my life. So, I accepted the fake name Javi gave me in the book (which I eventually had legally changed), I accepted the false narrative (which paid our bills and then some and catapulted Javi to super-star doctor status), and I accepted the fact that I was never going to remember or understand anything that had happened to me. We eventually had the conversation about marriage and kids and decided that we were fine and happy doing exactly what we were doing, which I also accepted. Javi got another grant from the college and started up another clinical trial. He quit his job at the clinic and stopped teaching so that he could focus on his research and public appearance lifestyle.

But of course, Javi couldn't let my shit go, which is why he consistently third-degrees me, and for as long as we're together, his quest will go on. He can't live with the fact that he wasn't able to fix me—wasn't able to find my treasure. Sure, he got *a* treasure, albeit through duplicitous means, but he wasn't able to open up the center, the core, the kernel of my story.

And neither have I...

My memory is hazy at best. Like, I remember 1984 as if it were a dream. I remember Kit and the rest of them, and all the shit about Ricky Kasso and the murder in the woods. I remember my boyfriend, Seth, hanging out with all of them, and talking crazy stuff. I vaguely remember playing with a Ouija board at Seth's house, and I vaguely remember that youth group they said we all used to go to. That night in the sump is locked. Like there's a big giant safe in my brain with a super strong combination that no one is able to crack.

Not even me. I remember being in the hospital. The psychiatric ward. And oh, do I have tales to tell from there! The judge mandated me to one year at first because of my mental state and the fact that Dan died (that was ruled an accidental overdose, but somehow, I was tied to it because of the cookies I'd provided that had an "undetermined substance linked to PCP" in them). They diagnosed me with some technical psychiatric thing. Said I had a history of mental issues too. And my behavior and mental state throughout the investigation and court trial warranted the judge to mandate his sentence. Kit, Seth, and Thomas all got probation for first offense possession. Then there was the wrongful death civil suit with Dan's parents and all, and because I was still deemed a loopty-loo, the judge tacked on two more years at the ward.

Kit and Seth came to visit me a bunch. My mother too. At first it was every week, but then, the visits dwindled down to nothing, and I haven't heard from any of them in years. By the second year of my stay, I was so zombified and comfortable in my routine, that I chose to stay longer. *Chose*—as in, voluntarily decided to remain institutionalized. *As long as they would keep me.* But by the end of my stay, the doctors all said I had progressed so well and come so far that there was no reason for me to be there any longer. Ultimately though, it's unimportant to where I am now and who I've become today. *Almost ten years later.*

I often replay these memories in my head throughout the day at some point, and I suddenly realize I need to stop reminiscing and seriously get on with my day. Live in the moment! Live in the present! I throw the covers off me, reach for my silky bathrobe, and pop up out of bed. I kinda feel refreshed, kinda feel groggy. It's a weird combo of sensations. Once I have my coffee, I'll be okay. I usually am.

In the kitchen, I check the fridge to see if I need to go shopping for dinner. I breathe a sigh of relief when I see a package of chicken defrosting on the shelf (Javi must have taken it out for me last night) and the brilliant colors of vegetables in the bottom crisper. "Chicken Teriyaki, it is!" I declare and shut the door. Once the coffee is done, I pour myself a mug, curl up on the couch with my favorite fuzzy blanket, turn on the TV, and flip through the channels.

Daytime talk.

Daytime talk.

Soap Opera.

Bullshit.

News.

And I pause my flipping because on the screen in a little box next to the newscaster's face is a picture of a pentagram and the words, "Ties to Satanic Cult?" written underneath. Something stirs within me. *Sparks*, if you will, and I turn up the volume to full blast.

"Thirty-year-old David Condry of Glendale is accused of murdering his landlord, 89-year-old Josephine Adinolfi."

Josephine?

As the newscaster says the name of the victim, it sounds gritty. Like she's not really saying it. Like it's someone else's voice. *Something* else's voice. Speaking directly to me.

Goosebumps rise on my arms, making the baby-fine hairs stand at attention, and my ears perk up with curiosity like a bloodhound catching a scent. I raise the volume because I think I hear music from the apartment above us and I don't want to miss a word of this broadcast.

"According to reports, Condry was discovered wearing a pendant in the shape of a pentagram, often a symbol indicating Satanic involvement. A photograph of a demonic face was found in his wallet with the words "Sisters Linked to Satanic Torture Kill" and "Human Sacrifice Would Open the Gates of Hell" printed on it. Adinolfi's grandson told police at the scene that it was no secret that Condry had a library filled with Satanic and occult literature but that he was an overall nice guy who kept to himself. Police are still investigating a possible motive for the killing."

The music from the upstairs apartment gets louder. I shut the TV off and bury my head in the couch pillow. My hands shake. My insides shake. Something about that news report hit me deeply, and I can't put my finger on the why. I want to get up from the couch, get my drawing pad and go out to the balcony, but I can't move. I physically can't get up! It's like I'm locked in place. *That poor woman*, I think. *That poor woman and her poor grandson.* I close my eyes and try to envision the murder scene and Condry with his hatchet standing over her old, feeble body. I don't know why I thought of a hatchet as the murder weapon—the news report never specified *how* he killed her or what he used to do it. It could have been a gun for all I know. A hatchet just feels right.

That's how I would have done it.

My stomach does a violent turn. *Why the hell did I think that? What the hell is wrong with me? Why can't I stop shaking?*

I think I'm having a major panic attack, and I need to call Javier. Only, I can't get up, I can't get up, I can't get up. I should have listened to him when he told me to get one of those mobile phones. Maybe we'll do that this weekend. I wish he would get home soon, but I know he won't; it's still the morning. My chest tightens a little. It's a little hard to breathe.

I'll just wait for him here.

And I hope the neighbors turn that music down by the time he gets home.

Chapter 13

Thursday, February 10th 1994
The Shoreline Apartment Complex
1700 Neilson Way APT #1010
Santa Monica, California
Night of the New Moon

" **J**o! Josie! Josephine! Are you okay?" Javi's voice is in the distance; it has been all day, and now I can vaguely make out his face in front of me, leaning over, snapping his fingers in my face. He looks fuzzy, like a staticy commercial coming through, and he reaches for my arm, grabs my wrist, and takes my pulse. "Jo!" he calls one last time, and he finally comes into full vision. I blink my eyes and he tunes in. He's really here and not some image on my TV.

"Babe! What the hell? Are you okay?"

I rub my eyes hard to help regain my focus. "Yeah. Yeah," I say quietly. "What time is it?"

"It's almost 11 p.m. It's late. Have you been here like this all day?"

"Eleven? Why are you home so late?"

Javi pauses for a second. "I had to work late—paperwork. But that's not important right now. What the hell happened here?"

I try to get up from the couch. "I... I don't know. I just kinda... oh shit! I never made dinner!"

He squeezes my wrist tighter, helping me to stand. "It's fine. It's fine. I picked up something to eat before I left work. I've been leaving you messages all day."

I open my mouth to respond, but a wave of dizziness sweeps over me, and my knees buckle from under me. Javi quickly throws his arm around my waist and prevents me from collapsing back onto the couch. "Okay, okay, girl. I got ya. Come on. Let's get you into the bed," and he clutches me closer and leads me into the bedroom.

He gets me settled under the covers, disappears into the kitchen, and comes back with a snack tray. There's half of a buttered bagel, a small bowl of cut up fruit, and a glass of orange juice. I open my mouth to protest the juice. *I mean, doesn't he know by now that I hate orange?* Before words come out, he says, "Eat some of this. Your sugar might be low. Did you eat anything all day? Can you tell me what happened? Why didn't you pick up the phone?" He batters me with his rapid-fire questions, but I'm still too hazy to completely process. I honestly don't have an answer for him because I'm still not quite sure exactly what happened. Then, he glances over to the nightstand, and his face nearly falls to the floor. "Your pills! Jo, you didn't take your pills!"

I look over, and sure enough, they're still there. "I... I... I don't know," I stammer. "I must have forgotten..."

"Jo!" he admonishes. "These are serious, heavy-duty medications! You can't just forget to take them!"

He scoops them up and drops the gems in my hand. *Blue round. Cylinder yellow. Squishy red. White horse (my least favorite).* Quickly, I gurgle them down with the juice.

"We'll have to adjust your time schedule now," he mutters under his breath with a sour and condescending tone, and I slump back into the pillows. I kinda hate when he talks to me *about* me. Like I'm not really *me*, if that makes sense. And he does it often. At first, I had just chalked it up to him being older and wiser, and it was almost endearing in a *Svengali* kind of way, but right now, I don't like how it makes me burn on the inside, like the pills are hard to swallow and so is Javi. I pick at the bagel and fruit for a few minutes before he snatches the snack tray from my lap and places another pill in my hand. "This will help you sleep. You look like shit, Jo. Maybe tomorrow you can explain everything. Now, you just need to rest."

I smile and dry swallow the pill. Javi rolls his eyes in a non-eye rolly way, walks to the answering machine, and presses play.

"*Hey Babe, it's just me,*" Javi's voice says. "Okay," he says to the floor, "that was the first time I called." He presses the button to advance the machine to the next message. Telemarketer. He presses again. Another telemarketer. "What's with these goddamn courtesy calls?"

"Not very courteous, are they?" I say with a chuckle; I can already feel the effects of the sleepy pill.

Javi just eyeballs me and goes to the next message. *"Josie girl, I just wanted to..."* his jovial voice comes on the machine again. "That was my second message. Were you on that couch the whole time? Did you go out today? Were you on the balcony and just didn't hear it?"

I shrug my shoulders. "I dunno. Hey, what in the fuck did you give me, anyway?"

Again, he presses the button. "Nothing, nothing, a sedative, just close your eyes."

"A sedative?" I squawk. "You gave me a sedative?"

"Yeah, yeah, yeah." He waves a hand dismissively at me and a blue trail follows behind it. *"Josie. I have some things I need to catch up on here at work,"* Javi's third message plays. His voice comes through the machine in shaky waves, or maybe I'm just altering the sound in my head because of the sedative?

"It's so late," I mumble.

"Yes, babe, it's late," he repeats. "Close your eyes and rest."

He presses the button a last time, and the beeping sound fills my head. I wince from the harsh tones of the mechanical buzzer as it penetrates the soft spots of my eardrums. Suddenly, a familiar voice rings clear, and I try my hardest to focus on it. It rouses me. Opens me. I struggle against the fast-acting drugs to perk up and pay attention. *"Joephie?"* the baby-doll voice says with heavy hesitation. *"Joephie, it's Kit. If you're there, please pick up."*

"Kit?" I drowsily repeat in disbelief. "Kit? Is that really you?"

"I… I know it's been a long time, but I really need to talk to you. It's important. Please call me back as soon as you can. It's doesn't matter what time it is." She leaves a number that I don't hear.

"She sounded so sad." I pucker out my bottom lip.

"She sounded urgent," Javi corrects.

"I'll call her back in the morning," I slur.

"Hmmm," he says pensively. "It's only 8:30 p.m. in New York. You should call her back now." There's an odd urgency in *his* voice that kinda gives me the creeps.

"Sure!" I exclaim and reach my arm to him for the phone, but it drops back down heavy to the bed. I'm really in no shape to do much of anything right now.

"Do you want *me* to call her back? I mean, it sounded like she really needed to talk to you."

You? Why you? She doesn't know you! Wouldn't that be super weird? I think, but the word, "Sure!" comes out of my mouth again.

He picks up the receiver, and I roll over onto my side.

I'll call Kit back in the morning and explain everything.

"Hello? My name is Dr. Javier Efrain Peterson," he says, turning on a strong accent on his Latino name. I've noticed that he only does that when he meets someone for the first time. "I'm Josephine's boyfriend. May I speak with Kit, please?"

My eyes flutter in the back of my head, and I don't get to hear what he said to her. But it's okay. He'll tell me all about it in the morning.

Friday, February 11th 1994
The Shoreline Apartment Complex
1700 Neilson Way APT #1010
Santa Monica, California
Mid-Afternoon

Javi tinkers in the kitchen. The sounds of the pots and pans clanging and clashing wake me from yet another dreamless night of sleep. He forcefully opens the drawers and unloads the dishwasher with such force that his anger and agitation is palpable down the hallway. It must be mid-afternoon. He let me sleep late, but he didn't really. Besides, what the hell is he doing home? It's Friday. He's usually off to the office by now. I stretch my arms above my head and let out a long, satisfying yawn. I plan to get up, shower, and get ready before I even engage him in conversation, but before I do any of that, gotta take those pills he left for me on the nightstand. I roll my eyes.

But before I even make a move to get out from under the covers, Javi marches into the bedroom and plops down at the foot of the bed. "You hear me yawn or something?" I joke, but his face is stone cold like a statue in the snow. "What's up?" I press. "You look like you lost your best friend or something." Still, his facial expression remains the same, and a chill runs through me.

"I spoke to your old friend, Kit, last night. Do you remember any of that?"

I nod. "Vaguely. I know I passed out hard when you got her on the phone. Weird that you called though. What happened?"

He puts his hand out and grabs my ankle. "Jo, I hate to tell you this but…" his voice trails off and my body stiffens.

Panic bubbles up in my stomach. "What? What happened?"

"Your mother passed away," he says reverently.

I freeze. Like hard ice encasing me. Everything stops—even the blood in my veins. My heart skips a beat because the blood can't pump through the thick layer of frost fast enough. I don't think I can move. I don't think I can even blink. Everything is hard and cold and detached…

…*And free.*

"Babe, I'm so sorry…" he tries to console.

"How?" I whisper. "How did it happen? How did she die?"

"They're calling it an accidental overdose."

Accidental overdose? I know I haven't seen or spoken to my mother in years, but I know she wasn't the type to get hooked on drugs. That wasn't Nancy's style. Cigarettes? Sure. The occasional glass of red wine or screwdriver? Why not? But drugs? Hardcore drugs? To the point of actually OD'ing? Doesn't make sense. "Suicide. That's code for suicide," I say flatly.

"No, it's not, Jo. There's no way to determine your mother's intent."

"Okay, Dr. Peterson," I say, the sarcasm dripping from my mouth like venom, "whatever you say."

He lowers his eyes, ignoring my comment. He pauses for a moment, giving me time to absorb and digest. I know this stage of his interrogation because I've been on this end of it for years now. His questioning and information disseminating techniques are pretty predictable now. "I know you didn't have a relationship with her or really any contact for that matter, but there are some things you're going to have to take care of."

"Wait, what?"

"Kit gave me all the information from the coroner. I'll take care of all the details for you, so you don't have to worry about a thing. I'll figure out the funeral arrangements and…"

"Funeral?"

"Or cremation. Whatever your mother wanted."

I throw the covers off me and jump out of the bed. "I have no idea what my mother wanted!" I scream.

Quickly, Javier gets up and holds me by the shoulders. "I'm sorry," he says gently, trying his best to calm me down. "I know this is a lot to take in, but I'm here for you. I'm going to help you every step of the way."

"How did Kit find me? Josephine Turner went off the grid ex-amount-of-years ago. She doesn't even exist! Josephine Childes is unlisted…"

And Josephine Adinolfi is dead.

"Kit said the police let her into your mother's house…"

"Oh fuck! The house!" I put my head in my hands and bend my body forward in desperation, and Javi rubs my back.

"We have plenty of time to figure out all her assets."

"Her assets? Like her car and her bank account, and…"

"The house."

I stand straight up and take a step away from him. "Fuck that! I don't want any of that. That part of my life is over."

"You're her next of kin, Josie. Her only heir. Her only family member. It's all yours whether you want it or not."

"Jesus Christ…"

"I told you I would take care of everything. I'll help you sort everything out when we get to New York."

My face twists something awful. "Get to New York? What are you talking about 'get to New York?'"

"I took the next week off from work," he explains. "I booked our tickets. We get into JFK tomorrow night. I rented a car for us to pick up at the airport, and we'll drive out to the house and…"

I can't believe what I'm hearing right now. Rage works its way up from the bottom of my feet all the way to the tips of my fingers. A surging power courses through me, and I feel like I could strike him down dead with sheer will. "Are you insane? What the fuck were you thinking, Jav!? How many fucking times have I told you I have zero desire to step foot in that house ever again? For fuck's sake!"

Javier makes a move to touch my arm, but I jerk away from him violently. "It'll be good for you," he says calmly, but his eyes report something different—something deeper. "It would do you some good to have closure. Mourning. You can finally lay that chapter of your life to rest."

"I already have laid that chapter to rest, Jav! I moved on long ago. I'm happy now in this life. Happy with us and the way we live. Happy with the distance I've created from everything in my past."

"Are you, though? And how can you call it distance when you can't even remember the crucial stuff?"

"I remember enough."

"I wouldn't call it distance, Josephine. I'd call it blocking it all out." He puts on his "doctor voice," the one reserved for when he feels powerful, like when he's making a breakthrough with a patient. The one he uses when the patient comes to some epic conclusion that they think they've achieved on their own, but it was actually through the power of his suggestion that got them to that point. Javier has tried for years to get me to go back to Northport to visit my mother, the house, my old friends, and my old stomping grounds. He told me so many times that walking the trail in the Aztakea Woods or going to the sumplands would somehow *spark* those long-lost memories and crack me open like a chicken egg on Easter. For all those years, I declined. I have absolutely no desire or need or want to go back. Call it fear, anxiety, apprehension, blah, blah, blah. Call it instinct. Self-preservation. Whatever. All I know is this: in the course of seven months, my life was completely upended in a maelstrom of haze and sex that ultimately resulted in the death of a friend (that I may or may not have had direct involvement with). This is all clear to me now—my mother's death is Javi's excuse for his own personal satisfaction. He wrote an ending to my story—a false one at that—and sold it to the highest bidder, but the truth is something he will always seek, and it eats him up all the time—the not knowing, the question marks, the "did she really have a Satanic ritual in the woods?"

Satanic ritual? No, no, no, no, my story has always been one of psychiatric deficiencies—bipolar, paranoid schizophrenia with possible parental neglect and abuse. "My mother said I was cursed by a witch," was the bridge piece of dialogue to the systemic psychological beatings from a parent who was a paranoid schizophrenic herself. The only mention of any Satanic ritual was my proximity to and knowledge of Ricky Kasso and the Knights of the Black Circle. I have never recalled such things, or felt such things...

Until now.

Images of the upside-down pentagram from yesterday's news report flash in my head. The newscaster said David Condry was a "disciple of Satan," and he believed that a human sacrifice would open the gates of hell. But did she really say that? I can't remember, but it stays with me. Lingers in my head, wanders in my brain, opens my mind to things that I know I know, things that I know are valid, true, pure, wonderful, and delicious, like a mouth—a ripple—opening wide in the sky with pulsing stars majestically dancing around it. I let the tingling sensation work its way deep into the very core of my veins, warming that layer of frost over my heart, and I am suddenly filled with a sense of urgency and excitement to return to the place I have avoided like the plague for years. I want to scream my acceptance of Javi's plan across the Pacific Ocean for all the world to hear me, but I remain poised and controlled.

"How would we even stay in my mother's house, Javi? Wouldn't there be like crime scene tape all over?"

"No, Jo. She's been dead for over two weeks. She's been on ice."

"And it took them *this* long to locate me?"

"Apparently so." He pauses and takes a deep breath. "So what do ya say, babe? Let's go to New York, say your goodbyes to your mother, get all the legal stuff squared away, maybe…" he pauses again for a second, "maybe if you're feeling up to it, we can do a walkabout of sorts. Ya know, catch up with your old friends."

"Revisit my old stomping grounds?"

His face brightens. "Exactly. Like a final closure."

"The final chapter. Act Three."

His face contorts in confusion at what I said, and he doesn't acknowledge it. "I can help you pack your bag if you like."

"Nope. I'm good," I say curtly.

"Wanna have something to eat?"

"Nope. I'm good," I repeat.

"Okay. Wanna talk about your mom's passing?"

I sigh heavily and look at Javi, but I don't really look at him—I look through him, past him, beyond him. Deep into a gray haze that encompasses his aura, like a smoke monster taunting me. I stare so long that my eyes start to water. Maybe he thinks they're tears for my mom. I don't know. I don't care. "Nope. I'm good."

He looks confused again as he turns away from me. "Okay, babe. Take your time with everything. Don't forget to take your pills, too."

I look at the nightstand. "Yep, you bet," I say with a smile, but after he walks out, I scoop them up in my hand, and flush them down the toilet.

Chapter 14

Sunday, February 12th 1994
Kohler's Funeral Home
3067 Sandy Hollow Road
Northport, Long Island, New York
Night of the Waxing Crescent Moon

J avier and I flew into JFK airport last night. We picked up our bags and the rental car and headed straight to my old house in Northport, Long Island on Harbor Hollow Road. We rode in silence the whole hour. Come to think of it, we flew pretty much in silence the entire trip too. I mean, there was an "excuse me," or a "can you pass me that magazine" every now and then, but for the most part, it wasn't a chat-fest. Javi had asked if I was hungry and if I wanted to stop at a drive thru or something. I turned it down because I really wasn't, but he said he needed to have a bite, so about half-way to the house, he stopped for burgers. Whatever. I was just anxious to get there and get to sleep. Get this shit over with. Be done with that part of my life for good.

It was definitely weird when I walked into the house. Mom had left everything the same—she still had the 1960s fake wood-look Formica table with the horrific scratches in the top, and my bedroom was exactly the same way I left it when I was sent to South Oaks. She never changed, evolved, or fixed the broken pieces of her shambled existence. During my sessions with Javi, I'd learned to accept the fact that my mother had some type of mental disability, which was the source of my own mental shortcomings. "It's hereditary. It's beyond your control, but you can put it in your control," Javi used to say as words of comfort. He said that to all his patients though, because it's believable and empowering. I believed it. Believe it.

The bed in my old room is a single, so Javi suggested we sleep in my mother's king-sized bed so that we would be more comfortable together. I told him it was okay if he wanted to sleep there alone, but he insisted he didn't want to leave me alone. The thought of sleeping in my mother's room kinda freaked me out, like, what if she'd died in that room? What if she'd died in that bed? Javi assured me that the police had found her body in the living room and that everything was fine. I relented, changed into my pajamas and climbed into my mother's bed with him. As soon as I cuddled up next to him, he was groping and grinding up against me, kissing my neck and being all lovey-dovey. I bet my body language wasn't encouraging his cause. I mean, he should have taken the hint when I put on a flannel night-shirt! But he can be very convincing when he wants to be—when he *needs* to be—and his sweet talk of, "I totally understand if you don't want to, you've gone through a lot these last few days, but just think how it will relax you, and I love you so much, I just want to be with you, and it's been like a week, Jo." And blah, blah, blah. So, I gave in to him. Took one for the proverbial team. When he was finished and asleep, I slithered out of the bed and wandered into my old room. I felt comforted there, surrounded by familiar things, and I felt my memory trying so hard to chug-chug-chug back into gear and crack open the locks of my brain-safe. I ended up sleeping in my old bed the rest of the night.

This morning, Javi took me to the hospital to identify my mother's body and fill out some paperwork. I did it all in a daze. Like it was all procedural with no emotion attached. Now, we're here at Kohler's Funeral Home, and the receptionist welcomed us into the parlor so that we could wait for the funeral director to come and go over all the arrangements for my mother's dead body. This is an actual home—an actual house, and this cozy waiting area is most likely what was once the original living room. It's decorated elegantly with a red checkered rug, some colonial style couches, and ornate picture frames hanging on the cream-colored walls. The fireplace in the center of the north wall burns bright and fills the space with extra warmth on this chilly New York morning—so much extra that I take my coat off and toss it onto the white couch next to me. I've never been inside a funeral home before, but from what I understand, the owners live upstairs, the downstairs is for business and services, and the basement is where they prep the bodies.

Prep the bodies.

Some reason that thought puts a smile on my face. Javi gives me a weird look, but I ignore him.

I hear a voice coming from down the hall, and I stand up in preparation to meet the director, but when she enters the room, my stomach does a flip-flop and I freeze in place. Kit's perfect mouth forms the shape of an "O" when she sees me and practically flings herself into my arms. We embrace for what feels like an eternity—our chests press together and lock in place, and the heat of her svelte figure radiates throughout my body, easing my initial shock. She pulls back and regards me at arm's length. "Joephie! I can't believe you're here," she gushes.

"No, I think it's more like, I can't believe *you're* here," I say, still confused.

Javi stands up to greet Kit. He extends his hand, and they shake. "Dr. Peterson?" she asks.

"Javier," he corrects. "And it's nice to finally put a face to the voice."

"Likewise," she smiles.

I give Javi a sideways stare of contempt as I start to piece together the puzzle. He notices my rage brewing and shifts into damage control-mode. "I wanted it to be a surprise," he says quickly.

Kit's face drops a little. "Oh, you didn't tell Joephie that this was my place?" she asks him suspiciously.

"No," I interject. "No, Javi kinda left that little detail out." I try my best to mask my sarcasm and agitation, but the both of them know me so well and on very different levels that I guess it's not so easy for me to hide.

Kit smiles wide, puts her hands in the air, and rotates her wrists quickly from side to side, "Well! Surprise!" she exclaims with a cute chuckle. Her sweet baby-doll voice coats my ears and soothes my soul. Takes me back to that special time when I was here and she was mine, and I remember, even though we were friends for a short six months, she was the greatest, best friend I've ever had in my entire life. A sharp pain hits me right above my left eye and something clicks in my brain. Like, one number of a combination lock switching into place...

"Katherine Kohler," I say to her with a smile.

"Yep. I'd introduce you to my other half, Frank, but he's away for the week."

I raise my eyebrows at her. "Funeral home?"

She sighs and shakes her head. "Yeah, you know how that goes. I guess my affinity for the weird and creepy just ran too deep," and she gives another little laugh that completely warms my heart. "Frank's family has been in the business for like, *ever*! When his dad, Old Man Kohler, passed away, Frank took over full time, and as his wife, I guess I was along for the ride." She gives another little laugh followed by a long sigh. "Lots of Kohler ghosts here. Lots of ghosts in general, here."

I'm so happy she was able to manage to *get* her shit together and *keep* her shit together after what went down with us. I take her in—absorb her with my eyes, inhale the vanilla aroma that surrounds her like she just stepped out of one of those frou-frou, girly bath and body stores at the mall. Her blonde hair is swirled up in the back of her head in a neatly twisted bun. Her makeup is done perfectly and her glossy lips shimmer in the dim light of the parlor. *I wonder what flavor she has on today?* She's also kept in great shape—a little thinner from our teenage years—her dark gray suit is perfectly tailored to her slender body. The jacket is only buttoned at the bottom, revealing a signature "Kit-pink" silk shirt underneath. She looks fantastic! She's perfect—a strong, no-nonsense businesswoman with an endearing cheerleader smile. Like, a total knockout.

Like a total fox.

An image of Kit's naked body flashes in my mind, and I imagine my tongue dancing against hers. *Like we've kissed before.*

Javi's mobile phone chirps in his pocket, snapping me out of my salacious thought. He pulls it out, extends the antennae, and says, "I'm gonna take this," before walking out.

"Oh, man." Kit gives an enamored sigh. "I gotta get me one of those."

I chuckle. "Yeah. Javi's been pushing for me to get one too. Says it's a safety thing or something, but I don't see the point. He uses his for work and everything, and I don't, so I'm not sure why I would need one when he can just reach me at the apartment whenever he has to get ahold of me."

"I'm so sorry about your mom, Joeph," she says, reaching for my hand.

I swallow hard. "It's okay," I say. "She and I always had a rocky relationship. I hadn't been in touch with her for years—since Javier published…"

"Still. She was your mother."

"How did you find out? How did you get my contact info?"

"Well," she points to herself, "resident funeral director. One of her neighbors called the police to report an odor…"

I don't know why, but I smile at the thought of my mother lying on the living room floor, her body slowly rotting. The gases building up within her causing her stomach to harden and distend. Her lips curling back and her gelatinous eyes sinking into the depths of her skull. I imagine her rigid fingers frozen in a clutch position, brittle and ready to snap off her wrists.

"I'm sorry," Kit apologizes, again.

"No, no, no. Continue," I urge.

"The officer called me to come down to the morgue to see what I could do, and when I saw her, I knew right away who it was. I told them of my personal connection and explained that she had an estranged daughter in California."

"Estranged. Such a nice word."

She gives me a half eye-roll. "That's when they agreed to let me go into the house, search through her stuff, and find your info."

"Gotcha," I say with a firm nod.

She doesn't respond, and we stand together in the parlor for a few seconds in an uncomfortable silence.

"I read your book, ya know," she finally says, her voice turning frosty.

I cock my head to the side. *Is she challenging me? Expecting an apology? Looking for an explanation?* "It's not my book. I didn't write it."

"Apparently, you didn't live it, either."

She knocks me off guard for a witty response. All I got is, "Most of it, I did."

"Yeah. Most of it. Just not the ending."

I shift my body weight to one side and place my hands on my hips in a defensive stance. "I don't want to argue with you, Kit. I just want to bury my mother and go the fuck back home. That's all I want to do." Because that's the whole truth. I don't want to be here. I don't want to play "remember-when." I don't want to dig up any lost bones or whatever bullshit game Javi thinks he's running on me.

"I'm sorry. I'm sorry. I'm not mad at you. I don't understand, but I kinda do. I understand that you had to do what you did to survive. You had to tell whatever version you remembered in order to close it out and move on."

Yeah. Of course, she would think that. I don't have the heart or the energy to tell her that Javi made the whole thing up.

"And it just felt kinda, I don't know, sleazy, that you profited off Dan's death…"

"Wait a second!" I interrupt. "I never mentioned anyone by name. Everyone was written as vaguely as possible, and I tried to piece it all together to protect you guys and…"

"I know, I know," she says, trying to calm me down. She pauses for a second, and suddenly, her face screws up as if she's had some major revelation. "Wait," she says slowly, "you really don't remember, do you?"

I inhale hard. It feels like my chest rises ten feet in front of me. "I do. Most of it. Some of it. Barely. Vaguely. Not really. No."

She puts her arm on my shoulder and guides me to the loveseat. The burning wood in the fireplace crackles and pops as I walk by.

Kit lays her hands on my knees in a gentle way, and it sends shivers up my back. I remember all the times we spent in the back seat of one of the guys' cars and we cuddled up together in a loving embrace. "I never thought I would see you again," she says softly. "When I heard you left South Oaks in '89, I thought for sure that was it."

"You'd stopped visiting me long before that though."

"Joeph, I couldn't. It was so hard. It wasn't you. I don't know, maybe it was all those drugs they had you hopped up on. I just couldn't stand to see you like that. And then Thomas was giving us shit, but it kinda made sense, and…" She sighs, and I know it's one of regret. It's written all over her face. "It was just so hard for us."

By "us," I know she means her and Seth.

"Do you still keep in touch with everyone?" I slyly pry.

"Yeah, you can say the gang's still together. Thomas and Carmen got married."

"No shit!" I say, genuinely surprised.

She giggles. "Yeah. They're really happy, believe it or not."

"Guess they got over their on-again-off-again tendencies."

"They grew up. Carmen teaches at Northport Prep, and Thomas works construction. They live over in the townhouse complex where the Aztakea Woods used to be."

"Used to be?"

"Yeah. The land was cleared away for housing. We all teased Thomas saying that he wanted to be close to Gary's ghost."

"Gary's ghost?" I repeat mindlessly, but the pain above my eye flares up and I hear another clicky sound in my head. Another combo number switched in position. I see an image of the woods, leaves scattered around a shallow grave, and poor Gary's mutilated body—a hunk of brown dried blood and rotting flesh. Unlike my mother, there wasn't even enough stomach to fill with gas and fluids, and there weren't any eyes left to sink back into his head.

"Never mind," she says softly. "I guess it's not really funny when you think about it."

"And Seth?" I finally inquire.

"His parents gave him the house on Whispering Woods, and they moved out to the Hamptons permanently."

"Oh…" I say lingering the word with a long "o" sound and giant pause in between. "Married?"

"Divorced."

"Oh. That's unfortunate."

A smirk creeps up on one side of Kit's mouth, and I give a little smile back.

The front door opens with a blast of winter wind, and Javi comes back in, but he's not alone. Another male voice booms in the foyer—laughing, light-hearted, really hitting it off with Javi.

"Be still my beating heart," the other man says when they walk into the room.

For a fraction of a second, my world stops turning on its axis. Another click goes off in my head…

Trent.

"Josephine Turner in the flesh."

I stand up, meeting him face to face.

"Jo, you remember Reverend Trent Blackwood?" Javi says taking his coat off. "Reverend Blackwood is going to be the officiant at your mother's service. I was finishing up my call when he came walking up the driveway and we got to talking."

Trent and I lock eyes in a stare. "Yes. We go back some."

"Yeah," Javi says nervously. "I am shocked at just how tight-knit this community is!"

"You could say that," Trent responds.

"New endeavor for you?" I ask, trying to scan his brain.

"I needed to move on from the youth group scene."

"Dead people are easier, I guess?"

"Easier than teenagers."

Kit stands up in an attempt to break up the mounting tension. "Dr. Peterson," she begins and walks to Javi's side.

"Javier," he corrects again.

"Javier," she repeats. "While Joephie and Trent catch up, why don't you and I go into my office and talk about the particulars for Nancy's funeral?"

"No funeral. Cremate her," I say.

Javi shakes his head. "Jo, you never said…"

"I'm saying it now. No funeral. No service. Just cremate her. Whatever it costs. Whatever needs to be done. Figure it out. You told me you'd help me with anything. Help me, Javi."

He eyes me up and down, looks to Trent, then back to me. "Of course," he says and follows Kit into a back room.

Trent and I continue to stare at each other. He reaches out and grabs my hands, holds them tight, brings them up to touch his chest. He breathes, but there is no exhale from his nose. No rise and fall of his chest. And no humanly thump under the fold of his black suit. He smiles and his teeth still illuminate the room—the fake glow of a pretender striving to be human. *A demon striving to be an angel.*

"I knew I would see you again," he says out loud, but in my head, he says, *"Be not afraid. You know I'm no demon, Joephie."*

I gasp. Out loud. Not only did he read my mind, but he *spoke* to me without using words!

I hear another click in my head, and I think I hear music in the distance. Trent's eyes are records spinning on a turn table. Spinning backward. Rewinding time. Pulling me deeply into some kind of memory. I hear the song, but it's not a song.

They're singing for you, he says to my core, but it's not his regular voice. It's a voice that I've heard before. Guttural. Grainy. Gritty. The needle scratching across the surface of the vinyl. It makes me dizzy. Turns me around. Spins me. Guides me to opening doors and gateways. I see them there, in the distance of my mind, and all I need to do is walk over and push.

"So if you're not going to have a public service for your mother, we have many other options for a private ceremony," he says out loud, keeping up appearances. *"This is the sixth and final point of your journey, my Joephiel. It won't be long before you remember. I promise, you will see."*

Trent and I sit together in silence until Javi and Kit come back into the waiting area. "All set?" I ask. I stand up and reach for our coats.

"All set," Javi nods.

"Javier took care of everything, Joephie. Everything's good. We're going to take care of your mother. No worries," Kit says.

I toss Javi his jacket. "I know you will."

"And everything set with a service?" Kit asks Trent.

"Josephine has requested direct cremation. Once we get a copy of the authorization papers from the hospital, we can move forward with the procedure."

"Oh," Kit says. "So will you be in town for a while?" she asks.

I open my mouth to reply, but Javi beats me to it. "A few days. To sort everything out."

"Listen," she says, "everyone is getting together at Seth's house on Tuesday night. I don't know. They tape football shit off TV on the weekends and like to analyze it together. Strange male rituals." She quickly looks to Javi. "Uh, no offense."

Oh, so they do all still hang out on the regular?

"You guys should stop by. Catch up with the old crew. Have a beer or two. Or a Zima. Whatever you prefer."

I scrunch up my nose and stick out my tongue. "Carmen. She always liked those bitch drinks."

Kit and I laugh, and Javi just stares at me. "Seriously, though," she continues, "you should come. It would be nice to catch up with everyone."

She reaches into her inner jacket pocket and hands me her business card.

I take her card and flip it over a few times inspecting it mindlessly. "Sounds good. I'll let you know." I put her card in my pocket and slip my jacket on. "Thank you, Kit. Really. For all this."

She nods reverently. "Of course, Joephie. Any time."

"Kit," Javi says, heartily shaking her hand. "Reverend," he says, moving to shake Trent's. "Thank you so very much for your time during this tragedy. We will be in touch."

Trent shakes Javi's hand with the same fervor. "Anything you guys need. Even though a lot of time has passed, we still consider Josephine part of our little family."

"Thank you. Thank you."

"And remember, keep your good thoughts flowing and your actions to match!"

Javi smiles one last time as they disengage their handshake. He zippers up his coat, puts his arm around my shoulder, and ushers me out of the funeral home.

Chapter 15

Tuesday, February 15th 1994
Seth's House
95 Whispering Woods Drive
Northport, Long Island, New York
Night of the Waxing Crescent Moon

My finger slides off the button of Seth's doorbell, not able to give it a full doorbell-ring-push. The bell sound on the inside just does a "ding" rather than a "ding-dong," and already, I feel stupid and small and want to race to our rent-a-car and drive straight back to Santa Monica.

"You okay?" Javi asks from the side of his mouth.

I inhale deeply. "Yeah, yeah. I'm fine." But I'm not. I know I'm not. He knows I'm not. I must look like a crazy, jittery, psychopath right now.

No one comes to the door. I can hear voices from inside the house … and the TV is on … and there's laughter and all … and I know the bell rang at least once because my finger slipped, I heard the "ding", and I…

"Breathe, Jo. Breathe," Javi says, rubbing my back.

I breathe in again through my nose and exhale through my mouth, just like he taught me.

"Fuck it. No one's coming," I start to say and begin to pull away from Jav's touch.

Suddenly, the porchlight flicks on; a figure pulls back the front window curtain, peeks out, then opens the door.

It's Seth.

Our eyes lock when he greets us at the door, and a soft smile forms on his handsome face. My stomach bubbles with those old feelings of an old crush—like the kind people get when they're with someone for the first time and there's all that wonderful and uncertain anticipation. It's that feeling as if excitement and dread got married and had a baby and that baby was living in the center of their chest.

"Joephie," he says breathlessly, like he's seeing me for the first time in ten years.

Because it is the first time in ten years, you idiot!

"Hey," I manage to squeak out, and he moves aside from the doorway and signals for us to come in. "This… this is my boyfriend, Javier."

Javi reaches out his hand. "Pleasure to meet you."

"Likewise, likewise," Seth says genuinely. "Here, let me take your coats. Go on in. Everyone's in the kitchen."

I remember the set-up of his house very well, and not much has changed in the last ten years.

In my seventeen-year-old brain, Seth's home was probably the largest home I'd ever been in. To me, it looked like a palace from a medieval fairy tale. But now, it comes off as just a house. Comparatively speaking, my 10th story luxury apartment with the floor to ceiling windows overlooking the vastness of the Pacific Ocean is more open and stunning than this more than one-hundred-year-old dwelling. I guess it's all about perspective, eh?

We make our way into the kitchen, and Kit jumps up from the table to greet us. "Joeph! Javier!" she sings as she throws her arms around my neck and plants a giant swak on my cheek.

Thomas and Carmen are over by the stove, and they both nod at me. I nod back in acknowledgment. "Thomas, Carmen, this is Javier."

They nod at him, and Javi nods back as this awkward vibe settles in the room.

I shouldn't be here, I shouldn't be here, I shouldn't...

"You want something to drink?" Kit asks, deflecting the Thomas and Carmen weirdness.

"Beer's good," Javi says.

"Coke, please," I respond.

Kit smiles closed mouth and walks to the fridge. Seth comes in from the front foyer and eyes Thomas. "We're very sorry to hear about your mom, Joephie," Seth says, placing a hand on my shoulder. Goosebumps rise on my arms when he touches me, and I think I blush. I don't know. I can't be sure.

"Yeah. Totally sucks," Carmen chimes.

"Thanks, guys. It is what it is, right? We hadn't been in touch for such a long time. I didn't even know she had a problem and…"

Kit hands me a bottle of Coke, and I chug it back to stop from blabbering. I don't know why, but I'm so super nervous right now; it's ridiculous.

"Santa Barbara?" Thomas says, making a move to the table.

"No, no. Santa Monica," I correct.

"How is it out there on the west coast?" he asks. He sits down at the table, and I notice underneath his flannel long-sleeve that he's wearing a black t-shirt with the word Nirvana on it. Here he is, a 28-year-old man, and he still hasn't been able to give up his band attire. Apparently, he gave up heavy metal for grunge, but I guess in the long run, some things never change.

"It's beautiful," I gush. "Relaxing. Chill. It's just a completely different way of life." I move closer and grab the back of a chair to pull out so that I can sit down, but I stop frozen in my tracks when I see a Ouija board in the center of the table underneath the pendant lighting. Four unlit candles are positioned at the compass points of the board and the planchette is directly in the center. My heart flutters and my hands start to sweat again. I turn my head to Seth. "What's all this about?" I demand.

"What's the matter, Joeph?" Thomas snickers. "You don't wanna play with us?"

I snap my head back to Thomas and narrow my eyes at him as if I was throwing daggers at his head. A flash of red rage surges behind my eyes and a pain in the center of my forehead twinges.

Javier moves closer to me and puts his hand on my waist. "What's going on?" he asks me. The group, really, because he's truly the odd man out.

"Oh yeah," Thomas croons with sarcasm. "Obviously. Joephie didn't tell you about the Ouija board 'cause it wasn't in your book and all."

"Thomas," Kit painfully protests.

"I don't understand," Javi mumbles dim-wittedly.

"My house," Seth begins, "is rumored to be built on an old Indian burial ground."

"Native American," Javier corrects.

"Yeah, yeah, whatever," Seth says. "Anyway, years ago when we, ya know… *dabbled*…"

"Dabbled?" Javi repeats.

"We tried to contact spirits in the other realm to tell us where they were buried," Seth continues.

"Why would you want to know where they were buried?" Javi asks.

Kit jumps in. "Because we were young, dumb, and thought we were badasses for being involved in the occult." She waves her hands dismissively in the air at the word "occult."

"Yeah, the spooky shit was dangerous and fun," Carmen adds.

Javi looks at me. "It was?"

I look around the table at Kit, Thomas, Carmen, and Seth. I scan their faces with a knowing glare because at one point in time we were all part of something—something that was larger than us, more powerful than us. Even though I don't fully remember particulars, I have the memory that *something* connected us all. And even though shit got out of hand and went sideways, we were still in it together. I purse my lips and nod at Javi.

"Do you remember this, Jo?" he asks.

I sit down and everyone else moves to the table to have a seat. "Barely. Like it's there, but it's not. Does that make sense?" The wind blows against the house, and I glance out the picture window. Seth's property backs up to the tree line of the forest, and I remember the trees waving at me, calling to me. Silver-gray trees that danced and bent and bowed and said hello and...

"Why do you think Joephie can't remember certain things, Doc?" Carmen questions. "'Cause you say that *a lot* in the book."

"Well, when someone has a traumatic experience, the mind can sometimes... 'splinter,' for lack of a better word. Your brain sort of protects itself so it *can't* remember. Sometimes it can even create situations that didn't happen to make up for the missing pieces," Javi explains.

"C'mon, Car," Thomas teases. "The good doctor says that in the book! Chapter five, if I remember correctly. Jeez, guess you weren't paying attention! And you're a teacher?"

Carmen swats Thomas on the arm, and we all give a little chuckle. My laugh trails off with another gaze out to the forest.

"Hey Doc, do you think playing the game again could jumpstart some of her memories?" Thomas asks.

"Uh…" Javi says with hesitancy, "I mean, it's a harmless parlor game. We're adults. There's no real spiritual thing to it or anything. It was pretty common for kids in the early 80s to be curious about the occult. A lot of the music that came out of that time had Satanic overtones. The era was referred to as The Satanic Panic—a time of dark spiritual discovery, but it was all debunked."

Seth eyes me sharply, and I cast my gaze to the Ouija board so as to not lock eyes with his again. Trent's voice breaks into my mind. Something he said many years ago: *Everyone is so consumed with this Satanic Panic; they wouldn't notice the real thing if it burned an X on their heads.*

"What if we try to recreate that night?" Carmen says.

"I've always tried to get Jo to do walkabouts and such. To re-live her steps. To go back in time."

"Wow, what a homecoming this is," I say sarcastically, and everyone laughs again.

"No, it's very nice that your old friends are concerned about you," Javi reassures.

"It's been way too long," Thomas says gently.

"Way!" Kit emphasizes.

"Okay," I relent, and Thomas, Carmen, and Kit cheer.

Carmen lights the four candles around the board and Seth shuts out the light over the kitchen table. We sit in darkness, save for the glow from the flames. Everyone's face around the table shifts with the movements of the dancing flame, shadows casting eerie shapes under their eyes, noses, and mouths. Ghastly masks of darkness to set the tone. The wind howls again outside, and a pocket of leaves from a raked pile flies in the air.

"Spooooooky shit!" Thomas exclaims, and a vision of younger Thomas pops into my head. He truly hasn't changed.

"Hush!" Carmen admonishes him. "Remember, put your forefinger lightly on the indicator, no pushing or moving. Seth asks the questions 'cause it's his house, and he's the one initiating contact, but your energy is going to help to usher in the spirit."

"We're the bridge," I say without even thinking about the words.

Javier looks at me with a puzzled face.

"Exactly!" Carmen says. "The spirit uses us to connect."

"Pick a color, any color," Kit whispers, and yes, I remember—envision a color surrounding you so that you can get in the zone.

"You've obviously all done this many times before, haven't you?" Javi says.

"Knights of the Black Circle, baby," Seth proclaims, and Thomas high-fives him across the table. The exchange sends a memory like a flash-bang into my mind. Something so familiar, like something Thomas and Dan said the night of the original Ouija board incident.

Carmen looks at them sternly. "Really?"

Seth stiffens. "Sorry, sorry, go on."

"Yes, hon, continue," Thomas mumbles behind a smirk.

"Remember, one finger on the planchette. Don't attempt to move it or slide it. Just keep your forefinger gently in place. As always, this is Seth's house, so he does the questioning. Stay calm and quiet, and hopefully a spirit will join us."

"Oh, Spirit from the Beyond," Seth declares in a strong voice. "We seek your other-worldly power and knowledge. Is there a spirit present with us?"

Javi looks at me side eyed. Kit taps the side of my finger with hers, and everyone gives a small giggle, remembering old times, remembering the old script. Memories bubble up in all of us with a boiling sense of nostalgia taking us back to a moment in time that was exciting, dangerous, and fun.

My stomach sinks a little as I envision a yellow light glowing around my finger on the planchette, and I glance out the window one more time. The trees sing. It's a low and rumbly song, and I think I'm the only one who hears it. Their long limb arms point at me and point to the sky, trying to tell me something, but I don't understand.

"You are welcome here in our domain. Are we in the presence of a spirit?" Seth continues.

We all focus on the indicator to see if there's any movement, and a rush of energy swells up from my feet and into my arms. It's hot and fast and feels like it can swoop me up and levitate me in the chair. I close my eyes for a second and breathe in through my nose so as to try to push it down, force the feeling back to my toes, and stay seated.

The indicator moves a centimeter to the right, and I feel Javi tense up a little. Goosebumps bloom on my arm, and every blonde hair stands at attention. I look around the table at everyone's shadow mask, and flashes hit one by one, fast and furiously—*Bones. Seth's Death. Seth in the woods in the back yard, tied to a tree, blood-soaked clothes, crying out for his mother. The forest. The moon. The bones. Bones. Bones. Bones. Seth against the tree, guts spilling out. Ashes in the grass. A circle. A circle. A black burnt circle. Bodies on the ground.*

A small gasp escapes my mouth as my heart pounds against my chest. I try to suppress the feeling, the energy, the memory, the vision. It makes me swoon.

"Babe? You okay?" Javi whispers.

"Shhhhh!" Carmen scolds.

I nod at him. But I don't think I am.

"Is there a great and powerful entity present?" Seth asks again, and suddenly, the planchette begins to slide across the board to the upper left corner of "yes."

A push and pull feeling starts in my stomach and works its way into my upper chest, and suddenly, I'm weightless, like my whole body floats above the table and chair. I open my eyes and look down and see that, no, I, in fact am *not* levitating. But it feels like I am. Like I'm just an inch above the surface of the chair, and my once steady finger twitches uncontrollably over the indicator.

This has happened before…

"Spirit!" Seth exclaims. "Thank you for joining us. Are you from the last 200 years?"

The planchette glides to the upper right corner "no."

"Are you from the last 100 years?" he asks.

The planchette slides down and back over the "no."

Kit lets out an uncontrollable squeak, and someone kicks her under the table.

This has happened before…

Seth shifts in his chair and smiles. "Are you from the last fifty years?"

The indicator rotates over the "no."

"Are you from our time?" Carmen interrupts.

The planchette does its little sway-dance over the "no" again but starts to move down the center of the board to the letters. Thomas reads them out loud as the indicator spells out, "N … A … N … C … Y! Oh shit, Joephie! Looks like your momma's here with us!"

I jump up from the table, and my chair falls back to the floor. "What the fuck, Thomas?" I bark, my hands shaking.

Thomas and Carmen snicker.

"Seth? Kit? Are you fucking serious right now?"

Seth stares at the table, ashamed, and Kit looks at me with a pained expression. Javier stands up and moves toward me. "C'mon, Jo. Let's go."

Carmen flicks the lights on. "Awww, come on, Joeph! We were just having a laugh!"

"Fuck you. Fuck you, Thomas. Fuck all of you."

I storm toward the door with Javi behind me. I grab our coats on the way out.

We're halfway down the driveway when Kit explodes out the front door. "Wait, Joeph!"

"What? What the fuck, Kit? What do you want?"

"I'm sorry, Joephie," she pleads. "I'm so sorry. Thomas and Carmen are such fucking assholes. I had no idea they were gonna take it that far. I'm so sorry."

"Fine. Whatever," I say and open the car door.

"Wait! Please. Let me make it up to you. Let me take you and Javier out to dinner tomorrow night. We still have so much to catch up on."

"That sounds lovely, but..." Javier starts.

"Fine," I say curtly. "Fine."

We get in the car, and Javi backs out of the driveway. "What was that all about?" he asks as he turns onto the main road.

"Who knows? Revenge? Whatever. I don't fucking care anymore."

"Are you really going to see Kit tomorrow?"

"Whatever. Why not? Can't hurt at this point. She didn't have anything to do with what happened tonight."

"How do you know?"

"I just do. I just know. I know Kit. She wouldn't lie."

"Regardless of the prank, was there anything that you remembered?" he asks because really, at the end of the day, it's about him and his ultimate goal.

"No," I lie.

Because he's right. Regardless of the fucked-up prank with the fucked-up people from my fucked-up past, there's one thing very clear to me—I'm almost there. I can feel it. I'm on the verge of breaking through. *Like punching through a portal to the other side.* I can almost taste it. I'm on the precipice of harnessing an unbelievable power—controlling something that has been in me all this time.

And I can't wait to set it free...

Chapter 16

Wednesday, February 16th 1994
Giuseppe's Italian Bistro
145 Main Street
Northport, Long Island, New York
Night of the Waxing Crescent Moon

"The thing about the human brain is that it's so complex. So mysterious. Just when a person thinks they've got it all figured out, something happens and they're back at square one. Surgeons who have to deal with tumors and other ailments; they need to be on the top of their game because of the complexity and fragility of the brain, because they deal with the hardware of the computer system. The psychiatrists and psychologists deal with the programming of the brain—'the software.'"

I twirl my spaghetti on my fork and stare out the front window of the Italian restaurant, counting the cars going by, watching the people stroll up and down Main Street, and detaching myself from my dinner companions just enough to tune back in to the conversation if called upon. Javier has his captive audience right now—Kit nods and smiles, interjects when appropriate, asks questions when appropriate, sips her wine, and flashes her white smile ever so often. Javi gobbles up the attention she gives like a sponge moving across a saturated tabletop. So I take a back seat to his pontification session. I know I shouldn't think that. He works hard and is proud of his career accomplishments, as he should be. He deserves every ounce of recognition he gets in his field because he's helped so many people. Maybe not in the most honest of ways, like in my case, but overall, he's a sweet man with good intentions, and I am extremely grateful for his love and support.

So why am I so incredibly bored and annoyed right now?

Kit turns her attention to her veal parmesan for a moment, and I can actually feel her screaming on the inside for Javier to shut the hell up. I give a slight chuckle, and Javi turns to me and says, "You okay? Not hungry?"

"No, no," I lie. "I'm just really tired. Distracted."

"Of course you are. It's been a hectic few days." He reaches into my pocket, and from underneath the table, he grabs my hand and puts in my palm, my shiny little friends. "You should take them now," he says with a doctor smile.

Kit watches this exchange between us and gives me a puzzled look. My fingers close over the pills, and I move my hand up to my mouth, pop them in, and chug some water ending with an "ahhh." Nonchalantly, though, I ease my hand and put the pills under my thigh. Sleight of hand. The Joephie Disappearing Act Part Seven! What Javi doesn't know won't hurt him. What Joephie doesn't take won't hurt her either. Because I gotta say, I feel so much better since I stopped taking them the other night.

"I'm so glad you called, Joeph," Kit says. "I'm really happy that you're here and that we can catch up like this."

"Same," I say and sip my wine.

She turns to Javi and says, "Ya know, I read the book." The tension among us builds, thickens, pulling back the blanket of chitchats and "remember-whens." I guess that's what ten years will do to ya. Ten years of unanswered questions, needed explanations, dreamless nights, sedatives, sleeping pills, and... and...

A gulping noise croaks its way from Javi's throat as his bulging Adam's apple moves up and down. "I figured you all would have," he says confidently, proudly, ready to pounce and defend his work however necessary. "And I'm sure you noted that no one was mentioned by name. Everyone was protected."

Kit sits straight up in the booth, her back stiffened in a defensive pose. "Absolutely," she responds.

"And I'm sure you also noticed the disclaimer at the beginning of the book that uses the word "inconclusive" to wrap up my findings, thus freeing myself and Jo from any misdoings."

Kit's shoulders slump forward a fraction of an inch for just a split second. I don't think she even realized that it happened, but it did. The body language of defeat. "Yes, but..." she begins.

"I want to go back," I interrupt. "I want to go to the sump."

Javi's eyes go wide with surprise. "Are you serious, Jo?"

Kit looks back and forth between me and Javi. "Joeph, do you really think that's a good idea and all? I mean, after what happened last night..."

"I've been thinking about it for a little while now, and I just, I don't know... I have this urgency to go back there. Does that make sense? I need to remember my side of what happened. What really happened."

"Joephie, we could just go back to my house, and I could talk you through it. You don't have to go back there. *I* haven't even been back there."

"No, Kit. If it were that easy, I would have picked up the phone years ago and just asked you to tell me. But what good would that do? You were as fucked up as I was, and I need to remember how it played out for *me*, from my vantage point."

"I think a walkabout is a great idea," Javi interjects. He turns to Kit. "I've been trying to get her to agree to doing that for years. There's something to be said for physical displacement. Being back at the scene of the trauma can work wonders for the mind. I could add an addendum to the book and…"

"Do you want me to go with you?" she asks.

"Only if you want to."

She picks her napkin off her lap and slams it onto the table. "Alright! Let me pay the check, and we'll be on our way."

Kit drives us over to the sumpland—that crazy swathe of Earth that was indented in the ground like God had tried to smash a giant bug with his thumb and left a gash in His wake. She parks, and we walk the path beyond the trees and reach the clearing where the six of us had gathered that fateful night. The winter sky is clear and rife with stars and the crescent moon is like a sideways smile in the sky.

Like a mouth trying to open up and swallow me whole.

As we get closer to the clearing, my head gets fuzzy, like static between my eyes and down the bridge of my nose tingling the entire circumference of my face. "Seth had a radio, right?"

"Yep. And Trent gave you that weird tape with that song."

I close my eyes and listen hard. The wind picks up and blows the trees back and forth, but in the shuffling of the leaves, I can hear it! I hear the sound, the song, the ancient music that lulled me, calmed me, empowered me. "I remember," I whisper to myself, but Javi looks at me suspiciously.

"Here," Kit says when she reaches the center spot. But she doesn't have to say it. I already know. Above her, I see a ripple in the sky. An opening, like a tear trying to push through the cosmos, but it's inactive. It tries to sputter back to life, to reignite, but it can't. There's no longer a power source to kickstart it open.

I saunter closer to where she stands, and in the shadows on the ground, there appears to be a black circle, like burnt grass or dark leaves spewed about. A surge of energy washes over me, like I've stepped back in time.

Through a portal.

The music gets louder in my head, and when I look at Kit, her face changes—like I'm looking at her through a kaleidoscope. Her visage transforms back to that night, and a flash in my head sends me an image.

A kiss.

"Anything coming back to you?" Javi asks.

"A little. Not much," I lie. I lie because it's not for him to know. Yet. But the reality of it is that it's all coming back to me, like puzzle pieces fitting into place. Up close, the image is distorted and blurry, but as you take a step back, the picture comes into clear vision.

And it's so beautiful.

I reach out my hands for Kit, and she intertwines her fingers in mine. With eyes closed and a sidestep of my hip, I fling her around the circle counterclockwise with me.

One time—I was blessed by an ancient witch while still in my mother's womb. The blessing manifested the day of my birth. The six. The six. The six.

Two times—Blodheksa. Blood Witch. The music that cracks me wide and open, igniting the witch's original spell.

Three times—"Seth's death"—the message in the board and my complete dominance over the physical world at that point in time. I manipulated it, manipulated them. Consciously owned my power for the first time and created an effect on the world.

Four times—Walpurgis Night at the Amityville Horror House. The first time I saw the ripple in the sky, I knew I needed to find a way to tear it wide open.

Five times—Seeing Gary's body in the Aztakea Woods—the nightmarish hunk of meat that filled me with wonder and awe.

Six times—The night in the sump. The five points of the star. We were the true Black Circle that night with a connection so powerful, the world almost split in two. *Dan didn't die in the circle. He died later in the hospital that night.* Had he died when I wanted him to, when I needed him to, this world would have been a better place.

The six points in time that Trent promised I would see.

And now, my mother's death finally frees me from the shackles of human connection. My life-giver no longer has life. I have no ties. My power can rise above.

Kit twirls and swirls with me as a glittery haze forms around us. She smiles and laughs, and on our sixth go around, she pulls hard on my arms, forcing us to a stop.

"That never happened!" she laughs.

"No, it didn't," I answer, pulling her close to me.

She bites her lower lip and gazes dreamily into my eyes. *You remember this don't you?* I ask her silently, and she nods under my thrall. It's her. In my mind, I turn her into the Kit from that night. The beautiful, peaches and cream skinned, raspberry-flavored lips Kit. I take her face into my hands and kiss her hard. She accepts my tongue in her mouth, and we roll them over and over like a Ferris wheel on a loop. Like a record spinning endlessly on a turntable. Her teeth graze my bottom lip and with one final click to the safe in my brain, the memories come rushing back as a surging flash of heat moistens the crevice between my legs.

I remember everything.

"Wait a second! Wait a second!" Javier exclaims, his voice breaking into our magic kiss.

Kit pulls her head back slightly. "Oh, yeah. I remember that happening." She smiles.

Javi's discomfort is obvious. "Josie, you remember doing that with her?"

I nod. "And the others."

"The others? The others? You mean the others in the group that night? Are you saying... are you...?" he stutters, trying to find the proper and clinical words. "Are you saying you all..."

"Fucked?" Kit finishes and laughs. "Well, except for Carmen."

I pump my palm in the air signaling to her that it's alright, to chill a little. "Yeah," I say to Javi. "We kinda were all *together*, for lack of a better term."

"And you're just remembering this now?" he says accusingly.

"Yes. I promise."

"I never forgot," Kit whispers, and I playfully nudge her arm.

"What else?" Javi presses. "What else is coming back?"

"Nothing," I lie again. "That's pretty much all I got."

Kit sighs.

You probably should be heading back now, I say to her mind.

"Well, I probably should get going back," she says, and I wave my hand at her, breaking my hold, snapping her back into her current self. She shakes her head, dazed for a second, and runs her hands down the sides of her tight jeans. "How long are you staying in town?"

"Our flight leaves tomorrow," Javi says.

"Actually," I say, overriding him, "I was planning on staying until the crematorium returned my mother's ashes."

He pulls at my coat sleeve. "Jo, we never discussed that," he pleads.

"Well, I guess we can discuss it now."

"Oh, well, uh," Kit stammers, deflecting the cold stare Javi gives me. "I would really love to see you again before you leave."

"Absolutely. I'll be in touch."

"Do you guys want a lift back to your house?"

"Nah, we're good. We'll walk it back."

"Okay. Talk soon." Kit turns on her heels and disappears up the path to the patch of woods.

Javi clutches my shoulder and spins me around to face him. "Wanna explain what happened here? I mean, if you had a major memory breakthrough, you really need to tell me." His tone is mixed—curious and annoyed, exhilarated and disgusted.

"Are you mad at something?" I ask.

"No, no… not mad…"

I take a step closer to him, bridging a little of the space between us, but he steps back up against one of the trees. "Are you a little jealous?" I ask. I close in on him, but he's trapped against the tree.

Stay.

"Jealous?" he huffs. "I'm not jealous." He tries to swipe his hand through his hair, but he's stuck. Pinned. A wave of terror comes across his face when he realizes he can't move. "Josephine? What the fuck?"

I inch in closer, nose to nose. I dip my head and bite his lower lip. He gasps slightly, trying his hardest to stifle his excitement—afraid that a dark piece of him will bubble up to the surface and explode into madness.

Like we did that night.

Slowly, I move my left hand down the front of his body and brush up against his crotch area. As suspected, he's throbbing through the thick denim. Slowly, I snake my right hand underneath the length of his coat and unbuckle his belt, snap open the button of his jeans, and slide the zipper down.

"What are you doing, Jo?" he asks mindlessly. "What is all this?"

"You'll see," I answer, and in one hard tug, I forcefully jerk his pants and boxers down to his ankles, exposing his thick cock to the frigid winter air. I cradle it in my hands, rubbing it back and forth, keeping it warm a few moments before I fall to my knees and take the full girth of him into my mouth. He tries desperately to thrust himself into the back of my throat, but he's paralyzed. The struggle is so interesting to see—he enjoys being dominated but strives for control. His body clearly enjoys the sensation of my warm mouth sliding up and down on him, priming him for the pinnacle release, but his mind strives to understand the spell he's under.

"Oh my God, Jo! What are you doing?" he moans, but I continue to bob my head up and down upon him. Quick, quick, slow. Quick, quick, slow. Taking him in as far as I can, lapping my tongue on the bottom side of his shaft, and grazing my teeth against the underside of his head. "Oh, God! Oh, God!" he moans again, letting me know he's close to fruition.

I pull my head back, releasing his cock from my mouth, leaving him on the verge of release. I reach into my back pocket and pull out a pocketknife and slice his inner thigh with an upward motion. He screams in agony, "What the fuck? What the fuck are you doing?"

Off my knees, I drive the knife into his stomach—one, two, three, four, five, six times. Six small cuts, but deep enough to allow the blood to gush out. My hands are covered in his crimson substance. Javier tries to buck from the pain, but he can't. He screams, cries, begs and pleads, "Why? Why? Why?"

I look to the sky, and much to my dismay, the portal remains inactive. A flitter, a flutter, a spitter, a sputter, but not enough to burst wide open.

The source is gone from this place, the guttural voice sings in my head.

But I need to try one last thing before I end the vision. I run the blade of the knife across Javier's neck. Ear to ear. The flesh splits open with a ripping sound like I imagined when my portal would tear open in the sky. The initial slice sprays my face in a fountain of red, and I extend my tongue to taste his metallic flavor. The knife slips out of my hand and disappears in a pile of leaves. Javier goes white, and he tries to call for me, but he can't. My blade tore his cords to shreds and all he can do is gurgle his last breath. He spits and chokes, and he is painted in red. His red. His own red. I watch until his eyes roll into the back of his head, and he cough one final time, but the source from this place is gone. My portal remains dormant.

Release.

Javier opens his eyes in a panic. He bends over, hands on knees, and vomits into the grass. I sit a few feet away from him, knees to my chest, leaning on my locked arms behind me. "Babe?" I call over. "You okay?" I smirk.

He finishes being sick and slumps down into the pile of leaves at the base of the tree. Confused. Upset. Scared. Unable to rectify the real bodily sensations of the unfinished blowjob with the visions I sent to his mind of his presumed gruesome murder.

"Don't worry, Jav. You're fine."

His eyes go wide and he claws at his neck, searching frantically for the gaping wound.

"Babe!" I plead, "I said it's okay. I just needed to see something. It's fine."

And what I saw was the inactive portal in the sump, and I know exactly where to find one that's alive and awake, waiting for me to punch through.

Chapter 17

Friday, February 18th 1994
Seth's House
95 Whispering Woods Drive
Northport, Long Island, New York
Night of the Half Moon

J avi drives me over to Seth's house. I told
him that I wanted to clear the air with my
old people before we headed back out to Santa
Monica tomorrow. It was some thinly-veiled bullshit excuse that a fourth grader would have been
able to see through, but my dominion over him
gets stronger each day, so it doesn't really take
much effort to convince him to do the things I
want. When he asked me why I was bringing a
plastic bag filled with my mother's ashes, I told
him it was because I wanted to keep her close by,
that it was hard to let her go. The absolute lamest
excuse of my life, but I guess he's so deep under
my thrall that it doesn't matter. He even agreed
to stay put in the car until I was done!

Seth is surprised to see me when he answers the door. Surprised. Embarrassed. Upset. All of the above. His cheeks flash with a pink blush of shame when he lets me in. "What's up, Joephie? I... I figured I would never see you again after the other night."

I nervously twist the plastic handles of the supermarket bag around my wrist. "Same. You guys got me real good, and..."

"I'm sorry," he interrupts. "I'm so sorry. It was Thomas's idea."

"I figured as much."

"No, I mean, it was Thomas's idea from like ten years ago. To do the Ouija board prank on you. After Dan died, we'd all gotten together, and Thomas was pissed as all get out. He came up with this master plan to fuck with your head. It sounded pretty good at the time and all... but putting it into action... well... not so much. I'm sorry. Please accept my apology."

"No worries," I say and reach for his hand. "I understand."

"For years we all wrestled with what happened that night. And Dan's death? It wasn't your fault. It wasn't any of our fault. We all equally had a hand in what happened."

If that's what helps you sleep at night, Seth.

"Yeah, yeah, sure, sure. I get it."

He squeezes my hand with genuine sincerity, and we lock eyes 'cause it's kinda our thing— it's a Seth and Joephie intense stare down that unwraps and unravels old feelings. "Please believe me when I say I wish things had happened differently."

Without saying a word, I squeeze back and send flashes of images to his mind—us flirting from across the room in the old church, fooling around in the sump for the first time, kissing in the car under the moonlight, late night conversations—like hazy Polaroid pictures flying by like leaves in the night wind. They rotate wildly starting from the ground, move up to meet his vision, then drift away on the breeze. He blinks his eyes as each memory hits him, and he smiles at each of them, but when they float away, sadness darkens his face. Looking at him is like looking at a cart on a Ferris wheel—up, up, up, down, down, down, smile, smile, smile, frown, frown, frown.

I must be smiling, too, because he gazes hard at me—at me, in me, through me, beyond the looking glass. "You remember everything, don't you?" He says with a smirk.

I let go of his hand and stop the memory transmission. "Of course, I do."

"I never forgot." He pulls me in for a hug, and I wrap my arms around his waist and up his back, pressing my hands against his shirt, feeling the contour of his shoulder blades as he slightly hunches down to meet my embrace. He's warm and comforting, just like I remember, and it feels as if he will swallow me whole within his clutch.

Swallow you whole like the portal in the sky widening its mouth to sing its power unto you. The gritty voice calls to me, and I pull back from Seth's grip. *Seth is the conduit.*

"Where's the doctor?" Seth asks nervously, as if he were coming out of some kind of trance.

"Oh, he's waiting in the car."

His face drops with surprise. "Uh… do you want to tell him to come in? 'Cause he can."

I chuckle. "No, no, no. I told him I would be quick. I just…" I stammer, trying to get the words out properly. "I just… I have something to tell you."

His face screws up with curiosity. "What? What's up?"

I pause, trying to find the right gut-punch moment to say what I have to say; I know the suspense is killing him, and I kinda like playing him like that in this moment, like we're on a cliff about to jump over together, and…

"Jesus Christ, Joeph, why don't you just stay?" he pleads, desperation coating his voice. "Tell homeboy to come in. We'll get pizza or something, I don't care. Whatever. There's so much we need to catch up on. I have so much I want to talk to you about. This is just weird and awkward, and…"

"I know where the bones are," I blurt, stopping Seth in his ramble.

He shakes his head in disbelief. "Wait. What?"

"The Indian bones. On the property."

"What do you mean? How do you know?"

"It doesn't matter how I know. I just know. I just needed to tell you before I went back to California, in case you were wondering and stuff."

"I'm not sure I understand," he says in a daze.

Yes, you do.

"But Joephie," he says as if he's responding to my mental insert comment, "what good would they do me now? It's not like we're in the Black Circle trying to open up a portal to hell."

We are the Black Circle. And it's not a portal to hell, per se...

"What did you say?" he asks.

I wave my hand in the air, making him forget the words he heard. "Nothing, nothing. But don't you think some big-wig archeologist would give you big bucks for a find like that?"

"It's possible..."

"Well, it's a one-time offer. Now or never. I can tell you where they are, or I can just leave. Hell, I'll even help you dig them up if you like!"

Because I need to pull them from the Earth in order for them to be mine. Like Ricky did...

He mulls it over. "I mean, I guess we could..."

You should go get a shovel.

"Alright. Meet me out back. I'll get a shovel from the garage."

I walk through the house, through the kitchen, and out to the back patio clutching the plastic bag, keeping its contents safe. A gallon Ziploc baggie holding my mother's ashes and a newly sharpened kitchen knife are nestled within. I open the back door and a gust of cold wind stings my face and hitches my breath in my throat. My heart stops for a second as I struggle to catch my breath. The silver trees at the edge of the forest wave and bow to me. Their branchy arms are tipped with burnt gold, the remnants of the dying winter. I reverently bow my head to them and listen for the song. It starts out in a low rumble and swells throughout the woods like a pulse to guide me to my treasure. X marks the spot. I tighten my grip on my supermarket bag as Seth comes up behind me.

"Ready?" I ask.

"Lead the way!" he exclaims.

The forest is dense with lightning rod trees and littered with brittle leaves that crunch beneath our feet with every step. The silver hue glitters against the falling sun on the horizon, and as we venture deeper into the woods, the pulse grows. It's like a magnetic vibe radiating from the Earth's core, humming in my head, leading me to the sacred space. The arms of the trees sway and point at me to go farther, deeper. We press on until I can no longer stand the hum in my ears and the heaviness in my arms and chest. The pressure builds so thick on the inside, I'm convinced my neck is going to burst at the sides—pop open and drain me of all my blood, choke me on my own life force.

We reach a small clearing and the earth rings loud, the trees laugh, the cold wind blasts the back of my neck, and a single crow lands on a silver tree branch. He caws. He has red eyes. He tells me I've reached my spot. "Here," I say to Seth and point to a space on the ground beneath the branch where the crow is perched.

"Are you sure?"

"Positive. Here, let me help you dig."

See, I'm helping you.

Seth drives the shovel into the cold earth, and in the reality that I've created in this sacred space, I'm digging too. But I'm not, really. I pull out the gallon bag of my mother's ashes, and in the clearing, I spread them around in the shape of a circle with a five-pointed star. After a little while, Seth's shovel hits something hard, and he says, "I think I found it!"

I fall to my knees beside him and reach deep into the hole, fishing around for the treasure. Electricity shoots up my arm when I touch a bone and draw it out of the ground. A femur, a tibia, a skeletal hand—something in me already knows the names, but I don't know the names, but I know them. I place them on the grass beside the hole, and Seth and I examine them. "Holy shit!" he marvels. "How did you…"

"I just knew," I repeat and hold up the femur. It's caked with dirt and a layer of oily substance coats the surface of the bone.

"We should clean them," he says. "Remember Ricky? When he dug up that colonial gravesite, they said he cleaned the bones with soap and peroxide, and then he bleached the skull so he could drink beer from it without getting sick."

"You should go back to the house," I say. "Call Thomas, Carmen, and Kit. Tell them to come over. Tell them where we are in the woods. I know they would love to see this."

"But..."

Go.

Seth stands and jogs back to the house while I sit and stare in wonder at the bones before me. I wipe them down, cleanse them, sterilize them until they shine and glisten in the half-moon light. Ricky needed chemicals and soaps to get his bones prepared, but I don't. I harness the power of the silver trees, the moonlight, and the pulsing magnetic force that radiates from the earth. The crow caws again. He tells me he is pleased, and when I look up to thank him, I see the portal has started to form in the sky, a little jagged sliver racing across the cosmos, but there all the same.

It has begun.

For he who opens the portal will be blessed with a mighty power—a power beyond compare. Greater than any mortal has ever known, says the crow. But it's not his crow voice. It's not Trent's voice either. It's an ancient voice, the one I heard long, long ago.

Bones. Ashes. Connectivity. Sacrifice. The recipe will culminate tonight. Ricky had it all wrong. He always seemed to be missing an ingredient or two...

I take off my clothes, unfazed by the frigid open air. The cold has no effect on the heat coursing through my veins, traveling throughout every inch of my body. I dip my thumb into my mother's ashes, draw gray circles up and down my forearms, and lie naked in the circle of ash—the cleansed bones on my bare stomach and the knife from my bag at my side.

Waiting for Seth.

Because it can only be Seth.

As my very first lover, Seth is the conduit.

Only his strength can withstand my body and soul. Where others have tried and failed, it was only with Seth that the gateway began to creak and widen.

His jaw nearly falls to the ground when he comes back to the clearing.

"Come into the circle," I say, and he obeys.

"I remember you," he says wide-eyed. "I know you."

He kneels down before me, hazy and dazed, still under my partial control, because my dominion over the conduit isn't one hundred percent guaranteed.

I place the bones on the ground. "Do you want to know me again?" I ask, sitting up to meet him.

He stares at me, but his eyes are glazed over, riddled with my spell. Riddled with control. And something inside me says that he must come to me of his own free will.

Release.

Seth shakes his head wildly back and forth. "Joephie? Joephie? What's going on? Are you? Are we?" He looks me up and down, like he's just awakened from a dream.

I twist my mouth to the side and shrug my shoulders. "Finishing what we started ten years ago?" I say, in more of a question than a statement.

The silence between us is deafening, and I cock my head up to the sky for signs of the growing portal. It hasn't changed or moved. The stars haven't shifted yet and a sense of dread works its way into my lungs. Seth stares at me—like how people look at a car accident. They want to see, but they don't want to see, but they keep looking because they're too curious to look away.

"Oh," he says, matter-of-factly.

"What do you think?" I ask, like a child looking for approval.

"What do *you* think?" he replies as he picks up the tibia and holds it up in the moonlight.

"Oh," I begin, but am stopped when he extends his arm and runs the bone up and down my thigh. Like electric shocks on my skin, energy from the bone pierces through to my muscles and organs making me twitch and writhe. I lie back down, and he slowly moves the bone across my stomach, inching it down to the crevice between my legs, smoothing it over the surface of my sex, teasing my opening with the ridged end. He taps at me, hovering on my nether lips, but never fully inserting the bone in. Just inching it close enough for it to get covered with my juice. He slides the bone down my inner thigh leaving the thin line of my honey glistening on my soft flesh. My sex aches, longing for the long, deep penetrating thrusts of the bone. Any bone actually.

We've done this before, I say to him.

I know, he replies.

I arch my back in anticipation, for the moment of full insertion, but it never comes. Instead, Seth puts the bone down, removes his clothing and lies next to me on his side. His hands frantically rub the length of my chest while he buries his head in the crook of my neck, kissing and licking and biting at me from ear to clavicle. He grabs my breasts, pinches my nipples between his fingers, makes me squeal in pain and delight. And when he kisses my mouth, hard and wet, I see stars. Like an explosion in my head disseminates a million light particles into the cosmos. Our tongues dance a furious dance—one of passion and knowing and… connectivity. Because we've connected before. Danced this dance before. And now is our time to open up the sky.

Seth is the conduit.

And the stars have shifted.

I reach my hand down in between Seth's legs and grip his bulging organ in my hand. He is hot to the touch, just like me, unaffected by the February night. I move him up and down, readying his cock, taking him right to the boundaries of pleasure. The ashes from my arms rub off on his flat chest, some speckles of it clumping in his chest hair.

He wriggles his hips away from me, and I release my hold on him. I pull my head back, and my eyes ask, "Why did you stop?"

He rolls me onto my side and bends my upper torso forward, so my backside is up against his stomach. He pretzels my legs, and I arch my hips to give him easy access to me. As the anticipation steadily builds and the tear in the sky widens, he wraps his arm across my fetal positioned body and reaches for the skeletal hand before he plunges himself deep inside me.

I moan at first entry, my insides screaming with the first-touch sensation, the ache between my legs now satiated and satisfied by Seth's hammering motions. He dips the skeleton hand down my front and uses the boney phalanges to tickle the outer region of my sex. Every nerve in my body is on fire. Every muscle twinges.

And I rise.

And Seth rises with me.

We levitate from the ground, getting closer and closer to the opening in the sky. Every stabbing motion of him inside me lifts us higher and higher. The crow caws his approval, and we are engulfed in a bright white light that flashes like a strobe light around us.

Bones. Ashes. Connectivity.

Seth and I are connected. Even when his cock slides gracefully, and grotesquely, in and out. When he's inside, I clamp down hard with my inner muscles. And when he slips out, when I let him leave for a millisecond, my body aches for him to return.

The fingers of the skeleton hand probe me. Pry apart my outer lips and try to go inside along with

Seth's organ. The tips of the bones rub against his cock, feeling the ridge of his head before he drives himself deep. We both chuckle at our third lover.

High above the treetops, I am all seeing. A man-made light flickers at the edge of the woods, and a voice travels up to my ears, "Josie? Josie?" it says.

Do not see me yet.

Because I'm almost there, the stars in the sky are ready to explode, and I'm at the line, at the edge. I taste ashes in my mouth and realize I'm now face down in the dirt, at the corner of the circle, my mother's ashes smeared on my lips, and Seth bucking wildly behind me, in me.

And. It. Just. Takes. One. More. Minute. To.

Release.

Together.

My body relaxes under his weight. "I think we have company," I say, and he rolls to the side.

"I called Thomas and Kit."

"No. It's not them yet." I jump up, get dressed, and race to the edge of the forest where Javier is bumbling around the dark with a flashlight.

"Javi?" I yell, when I get him in my sights.

"Josie? Josie? Are you okay?" he frantically screams rushing toward me.

"I'm fine. I'm fine," I assure, but he scoops me up into his arms and dangles me off the ground. Curious that the time pause I had placed on him was only temporary. Maybe I was just too wrapped up in the moment of Seth that I lost concentration and…

"I was so worried. You took so long. You never came out. Then, I knocked on Seth's door, but no one answered. I went around to the back of the house, but you weren't there. I got so scared. I called the police to report you missing, but I don't think they really took me seriously. And after the prank your 'friends,'" he uses air quotes to emphasize the word, "pulled the other night, I didn't know if they had more nefarious intentions."

"Javi, stop. Slow down. It's okay. I'm okay." I grab his wrists and tug down hard. "We found the bones."

He runs his hand through his black hair, like he's trying to make sense of the words. "What do you mean you found the bones?"

I raise an eyebrow and interlace a hand in his. "Come on. I'll show you." And I lead him into the forest.

Chapter 18

Friday, February 18th 1994
Site of the Indian Burial Ground
Seth's House
95 Whispering Woods Drive
Northport, Long Island, New York
Night of the Half Moon

I sense the arrival of the others, so I leave Javier and Seth at the circle in the clearing and race back to the spot where the forest backs up to Seth's property line.

They'll look to meet us there first.

Sure enough, just as I stumble out of the woods—dirtied, bloodied—Thomas, Carmen, and Kit enter from the side gate of Seth's property and hustle over to where I am.

Thomas glares at me with daggers in his eyes. "What's going on?" he barks.

"Jesus Christ, Joephie!" Kit says reaching out to touch my arm. "Where's your jacket? It's freezing out! And what the hell? You're filthy!"

"Is that… blood?" Carmen points to my pants.

"Yeah, yeah… Seth and I were digging, I cut my hand on the shovel handle and wiped it down my leg. No biggie. That's not the point," I say hurriedly. "We found the bones!"

"Yeah, that's what Seth said," Thomas says slowly. He's looking at me suspiciously, like he knows something is up. Like he doesn't trust me.

Well, he shouldn't.

Carmen turns to Kit. "Did Seth sound weird to you too? 'Cause it didn't really sound like *him* on the phone. He sounded *off*, right?"

Kit shakes her head like she's shooing Carmen away. Like she's saying, "don't talk to me right now."

"Oh, he's just exhausted from all the work we did today," I say, trying to cover up, but Thomas still glares. Hard.

"Where's Seth?" he demands, his voice cold and stern.

"With Javi. With the bones. Come on. I'll take you out there. This is finally the discovery we've been waiting for," I say to Carmen. "Now you don't have to worry about getting in trouble and losing your scholarship!" Carmen looks wearily to Thomas as I take Kit's hand and beckon them to follow me.

Walking back through the woods replenishes my energy, and I skip hand in hand with Kit through the dead leaves littered on the ground. We go crunching merrily along the path leading us back to the circle. I think I hum a chipper little tune. Thomas and Carmen stay close behind us.

When we finally get there—Javier and Seth stand frozen in place, each at one of the points of the star. The tibia is placed in front of Javi, and the femur is at Seth's feet. Thomas says "hi," to them, but they don't respond. They can't respond. Earlier, I had started a small fire in the center of the circle with some of the dead leaves and fallen tree branches. The hand is next to the open flame. Quickly, I usher Thomas, Carmen, and Kit to the other points of the circle.

"Is the Doc alright?" Kit asks.

"Yeah, Joeph, he's bleeding from the side of his head!" Carmen adds.

I wave my hand dismissively, ignoring their inquiry. "Okay, okay, check this out!" I say with fervor as I position my friends exactly where I need them. I pick up the hand in the center of the circle and walk over to Thomas. "Look at what came up from the ground!" I say, dangling the hand in front of his face.

His eyes go wide with curiosity, like a little kid from a movie discovering some secret underground lair. He reaches mindlessly for the tips of the fingers and rubs at the bones. I watch him closely as he feels the sticky leftover residue from my sex, and a puzzled look sweeps over his face. He looks at me, looks at the hand, and looks at me again like he knows what I've done with it. He knows where those fingers have been. I smirk and jerk the hand out of his reach.

Thomas tries to make a move forward, but he can't. I've locked him in place. I've locked them all in their places. A collective wave of panic sweeps over their faces when the three of them all realize simultaneously that they are in my circle now.

They are in my domain.

The opening mouth of the portal starts to sing. I breathe it in and am filled with a yellow light.

"Seth?" Carmen calls over, breaking my concentration. "Seth, are you okay?"

But Seth doesn't respond. He's silent and still, and won't have anything to say unless I allow it. Surprisingly, Javi gives a little moan in his stationary state, and my head snaps with fury to his direction. "Joephie?" Kit pleads. "Is Javier okay too?" Her voice is soft and desperate. My heart softens at the sound, and I nod at her.

I press the bone hand to my chest so that it can feel my heart beating. "Ya know," I say, circling the small fire, "the fire is kinda weak. And you guys must be so cold out here. But the wood was so damp and the leaves burn up so quickly." I sigh, feigning concern. "Thomas! Why don't you throw your socks in?"

Thomas eyes Carmen sharply. Tears pool at the corners of her dark brown eyes, and against the firelight, the shadows make them look like tidal waves hovering at the edge of the beach ready to swallow everything in its path—swallow her entire face in its salty wake. She's red now. Flashing red. Glowing red. Red aura orbits around Carmen's entire existence. It sparks and sputters with every emotion that surges through her—fear, guilt, despair, uncertainty. Thomas relents, bends over to remove his socks, and tosses them into the fire. The fire crackles back to life like mini explosions going off in the woods.

"Hmmm…" I say. "I'm not so sure that's going to be enough. What about your coat, Thomas? Why don't you put a sleeve into the fire?" I pick up the knife, dangle the plastic bag off my left wrist and walk up behind him. Carmen squeals in her throat and bucks her shoulders from side to side, trying to break free from her unseen shackles. "Here, let me help you with that," I purr in his ear as I run the knife down the side of his arm.

"Joephie," he begs, "what is this? What are you doing?"

I slowly move the knife alongside his neck and press the tip of the blade behind his ear. A thin line of his blood trickles out and the ripple in the sky laughs with me.

"It was funny the other night, wasn't it?" I taunt. "Funny to spell out my dead mother's name in the Ouija board."

"We were just fucking around, Joeph. It was a goof."

"Ohhh," I say. "A goof. Got it. So it had absolutely nothing to do with any kind of revenge or payback, right?"

"Joephie, stop!" Kit yells, but I ignore her.

"Maybe it goes far beyond what happened to Dan," I continue. "Maybe, if you'll be honest for just one second, maybe your fucked up mind has a thing against me because I wouldn't sleep with you!"

"Fuck you!" he spits.

I smile when I hit that nerve. "Did you ever tell your wife? About the time I turned you down in the sump? About the night Dan died, how you tried to fuck me and were too small and weak to get control? How your tongue left much to be desired and didn't please me at all?" The words spew from my mouth, but my voice sounds deep and guttural.

"Thomas?" Carmen cries in confusion.

"Shut the fuck up, bitch! I swear I'll fucking kill you!"

Swiftly, I pull his hair, jerking his head back and put the blade to his throat. Carmen and Kit scream, beg, and tell me, "No! Stop! Don't!" but their voices are just background static noise. I drop the knife to the ground and kick Thomas in the back of the knees, dropping him to the ground. He continues to struggle against me as I hold his head back with my left hand. He curses and yells while Carmen and Kit are still frantic in their spots. To shut him up, I pull out the plastic baggie from the supermarket bag with my right hand and dump my mother's remaining ashes onto his face. The gray layer of soot stings his eyes, coats the back of his throat, and he coughs and chokes as I yank harder on his neck.

"Damn straight, Nancy's here! She's here with you now and forever!"

I take the plastic supermarket bag, place it over Thomas's face, and secure it tightly around his neck. "Say you love Satan!" I scream as his body flails and wails in the half moonlight. "I can't hear you! Say you love Satan!" I pull him back harder and look up to the sky. The light from the ripple glows and grows! It intensifies, pulsates, fills me with an incredible blast of energy.

"Please, Joephie!" Kit screams. "You're killing him!"

Carmen cups her hands around her mouth. "Joephie! Stop! Kit called the police! They're on their way!"

I let go of the bag and Thomas flops forward. He removes the bag, gripping his neck and choking. "What did you say?" I ask calmly.

"Kit said she called the cops after Seth called her. She told them some shady shit was going on in the woods, and they said they would send a car to check it out."

Kit's eyes go wide.

"Did you?" I ask her.

"N... n... no! I don't know what she's..."

"Don't lie to me!" I scream. My voice shakes the trees to their core. They bow and twist and shudder in my presence as the sound carries up and through the portal.

It must be echoing on the other side of time by now.

Kit's eyes spill with tears. "I was so scared, Joephie. I didn't know what else to do. It didn't sound like Seth. It wasn't him. It wasn't right. I was worried something had happened to the both of you."

I lean into her, practically nose to nose. The scent of her raspberry lips catches in my nostrils, and I feel sorry for her. This beauty before me, my beautiful friend. She's surrounded in pale pink—the innocence of a blush, and I can't bring myself to, but I need to, but all I want to do is hold her in my arms and kiss her until her last breath flows into my lungs. "I was going to take you with me," I whisper. "But I'll deal with you later."

I turn on my heels, march back over to Thomas and pick up the knife.

"Oh Joephie! Please, please, Joephie!" Carmen screams, but it's too late, I'm already behind her, yanking back her hair, and slitting her throat. Like a busted sewer pipe, her blood initially sprays out hot for a second, then empties out in a whooshing gush down the front of her. She falls to her knees, struggling to yell for help, clawing at her opened neck. She looks down at her hands painted in her own blood, and the red aura that had once surrounded her dims as she falls forward and dies. The ends of her long brown hair catch the outer tongues of the fire—it crinkles up into a black spindly mass as the sizzling noise echoes among the trees and the burnt smell permeates our noses. Carmen's blood soaks the earth within her section of the circle and the ripple in the sky widens. I breathe in the frigid air and soak in the splendor of the exploding stars overhead.

Thomas wails into his ashy hands. "Oh God! Carmen! Carmen, no! Kit! Help! Seth! Seth! Can you hear me? Doc! Help us! Make this stop! Anyone!"

I saunter behind him again. "Say you love Satan."

He turns his head to look up at me, his face fraught with anxiety and dread. "This isn't a joke anymore, Joephie." Tears streak his face like water tunnels burrowing through an ash field.

"It never was a joke. Say you love Satan."

"I love Carmen! I love Carmen!" he screams.

"Say you love Satan," I repeat through gritted teeth.

"Joephie, stop! The Knights of the Black Circle doesn't exist anymore. They aren't real."

"I'd say this is pretty fucking real!" In one swift motion, I put the plastic bag over his head and twist it at the back, putting as much pressure as I can until he stops flailing around.

And the sky growls.

I'm feeding its hunger. Whetting its appetite. Nourishing it and making it stronger.

The screams in the forest sing like Christmas bells in church. Where there was one voice, there are now two. Javi has snapped out of my trance, and he and Kit scream, howl, beg, plead, cry, admonish me, and try so very hard to get me to stop.

But this is just the beginning.

"You…" I gurgle in a deep voice as I turn my attention to Javier. "All this time. All this time," I say standing in front of him, "you wanted to know. Needed to know. So badly, so badly. It wasn't enough for you to advise me, your patient. You needed to unlock me. Unlocking Josephine," I bark. "And still, that wasn't enough. You wanted to control, consume, create, and transform."

He tries to speak, to answer me, to answer for his crimes and misdeeds, but I put a finger against his lips to shush him. "And still, you do not know.

Still, you do not see. But you still want to. Still need to. Even after all that has happened." With both hands, I rub the sides of his face, smooth over his scruffy cheeks and lay my thumbs gently over his eyes, closing his lids.

"Now you see…" I say and press lightly on his eyeballs and send a flash of an image to his brain. *My hands wrapped around Dan's throat, trying to squeeze the life out of him.*

"Now you don't see…" I say, easing up.

"Now you see…" I press harder and send another flash to his brain. *Seth plunging into me from behind with the skeleton hand between my legs.* Javi jolts from the shock of my control—the image and the pain sent from my thumbs.

"Now you don't see…" And I relax my force.

Visions of burning sinners and devils, and visions of burning sinners and devils, and visions of burning sinners and devils, and…

"Now you see…" I press even harder and send him a flash of my naked body drenched in blood standing in the center of the Black Circle in the forest. Instead of the leaves littering the ground, random body parts are strewn at my feet. "Past, present, future," I hiss and jam my thumbs harder and deeper into his eye sockets. His horrifying screeches pierce the night and coat the air with a sound I never thought possible from his mouth. My thumbs sink deeper into his head—the warm gelatinous substance of his eyeballs squish under the force of my pressure as blood oozes from the corners of his lids. I force my way so deep—I thrust in and out of his face, fucking his sockets with my fingers. I go in so far, I hit the front of his skull. With one final stab, and one final scream, he falls to the ground with a thud.

And the ripple smiles.

I scurry for the knife again, and Kit squirms as I draw my attention to her. Beautiful Kit. Perfect Kit. Sweet, delicious, glossy-lipped Kit. I move closer to her, smelling around her like an animal picking up the scent of its prey. She's still pink—dancing all around her. I step into the boundaries of her blushy glow like invading someone's sacred space. She winces as I approach, but I raise my hand to calm her down. "I would have taken you with me, you know?" I say softly.

"What are you talking about?" she cries.

I hate to admit it, but it breaks my heart to see the tears falling from her eyes. Like she's disappointed in me. Afraid of me. I flash my white light into her head to make her see in a way that Javier refused—to make her feel me like the way she remembers.

"You're not well, Joephie. You need help. I saw you hide your pills under your leg at dinner the other night. How long have you been doing that? That's probably not good for your mind to just not take your medication. We need to call your doctor, Joseph. I can help you get better." She's frantic. Desperate.

"Why?" I respond. "I've never been better." I push her blonde hair away from her eyes—her perfectly coiffed bangs. *Some things never change.* In my mind, I lower the knife between her legs and insert it deep inside her until she comes to death, but I can't. Something snaps inside me. Something cries on the inside as I look at her. And I realize—she is the mirror, the reflection of who I could have been. In some alternate timeline, some alternate universe. She is the me from the opposite path. Kit's love for me was never about control, or sex, or belonging, or any other bullshitty excuse. Her love was innocent and pure. She was always true. She was always pink.

I stumble back and double over with a sharp pain in my stomach, and for that split second, that fraction of a moment, my hold on her is broken, and she goes running and screaming off into the woods, back in the direction of Seth's house.

And I let her go.

The crow squawks his displeasure.

"Shut up!" I snap at him.

My millisecond of weakness must have also undone my hold on Seth because he backs up against the nearest tree and moans my name.

"I'm here, Seth. I'm here," I say as I dip one shoulder under the crook of his arm to help steady him against the tree.

"They stopped screaming," he says, his voice shaky, like he'd been drinking all night.

"Yes, they did, didn't they?"

"And we found those bones! I knew they were here somewhere." He laughs.

"Yes. Yes we did." I press him up against the tree and look into his eyes.

He stares longingly at me, lovingly, like if we were in that alternate timeline we would have been happy and together. "I know you," he says, but it's not his voice. It's Trent's voice. But it's not Trent's voice. It's the guttural voice of the ancients singing to me through time and space. "It was always supposed to be you, like this."

Trent?

"No. But we're all connected, Joephie. Always have been."

"Always will be," I reply. And just like I knew it had to happen, just like I've seen it in my visions so many times before, I run the blade over Seth's lower stomach. His blood spills out and over my hand—hot and sticky, glopping between my fingers. The knife slips from my grasp and I squish my hands, reaching into his opened cavity. His entrails spill out at the base of the tree. The crow screeches with delight as Seth falls forward.

Seth's death.

And I rise. Levitate from the ground. Work my way up above and toward the mouth in the sky. It smiles at me. Invites me. Welcomes me. Wants to swallow me.

The portal sings and glows with magnificent light. The stars pulse like heartbeats in the sky—heartbeats that are in perfect time with my own steady rhythm. The ripple is open at full capacity, and it shines down and around me, through and in me, beyond me. I look up into the hole. Through the hole. I raise my arms and strive to touch it, strive to go into it. To be bathed in the power and the glory that is mine, now and forever. I am electrified with a constant ebb and flow of delicious orgasmic waves, but not just between my legs. I am filled everywhere in my body with pleasure, sin, darkness, and light. It radiates through me. Illuminates me. I am illuminated in both the physical, spiritual, emotional, and psychological sense. Power courses through my veins, as my human blood has dried up within them and is replaced with the power of the stars. The morning stars. The entire cosmos is at my beck and call. I can make mountains move and oceans stop. I can darken the sky at will and bend space and time. I have transcended. Ascended. Shed myself of my human shell. I am dizzy and drunk. The Blodheksa song fills the space in my head.

Say you love Satan.

I love you, Satan.

Say you love Satan.

I love…

As I rise higher to reach the portal, I have made peace with what I've become. With what I've done. Because now I am free from the chains of the human construct.

Now, I am in control.

I am control.

Yet, below me, lights flicker in the pockets of the woods. Left. Right. Center. They flash blue and white and red. They are not from me. I breathe in and disappointment creeps into my heart as I feel my body descend. I stretch to reach the opening of the portal, but it slips from my fingertips like I am being pulled back down to the earth. The Blodheksa song is now replaced by the singing of sirens and the barking of dogs. The portal lights wink at me and wave their hands goodbye. The stars fade to black, and the mouth slowly shuts tight.

But I have so much left to do. So much to do. So much to do!

I drift down closer to the earth, and I witness the full scope of what I've done—the bones, the ashes, the sacrifice—and I smile at my work. I smile that I was able to do what Ricky couldn't— open the portal and be bathed in the power.

I will complete it someday.

This fraction of time and space awakened my true power. Awakened me to fulfill the blessing that was bestowed upon me in the womb.

I reach the center of the circle, and I open my eyes to survey the land around me—blood-stained earth and lifeless bodies. The sirens grow louder, the lights flash closer, the dogs are within reach. I know it's only a matter of time. But for now, for this moment in time, I am in the Black Circle. I am one with the Black Circle.

I am the Witch of the Black Circle.

> *The Dawn of the Blood Witch* saga continues with a journey back to the time of The Salem Witch Trials in Massachusetts. Inspired by true events, *Witch of the Red Thorn* encounters some familiar faces while revealing critical aspects of the Blodheksa legend.

Book Club Questions

1. Have you ever experienced any "other worldly" encounters that could make you sympathize with Joephie?

2. How would you describe the energy around Trent's character? Did your feelings toward him change throughout the book?

3. Needs and wants are different things yet can sometimes be considered two sides of the same coin. Discuss the role of Kit in Joephie's life. What is the connection between the two? Did Joephie need her, want her, or both? And why her?

4. Is there any significance to the fact that Joephie and her friends are teens? How could her story have been different if these experiences had occurred deeper into her adulthood?

5. What is Javi's role in Joephie's growth? What is your take on his views of Joephie?

6. Nature seems to be a constant presence in Joephie's life. She often describes the moon and stars, the trees, the feeling of the air

and darkness. How is nature significant in Joephie's experiences?

7. Sexual encounters are intertwined with Joephie's other experiences. How is sex important in Joephie's awakening as well as the opening of the portal?

8. Throughout the book, Joephie repeats her mother's words that she "was cursed by a witch." Chapter 11 reveals the truth of her past. How does this change or not change your view of Joephie (or her mother)?

9. Throughout history, people have commonly attributed witchcraft to the devil's presence or mental illness. What are your thoughts on this?

10. Do you believe in witches/witchcraft? If not, has reading this book made you reconsider any aspect of it? Why or why not?

11. If you have read any of the other books in the series, how was this similar or different to the others? What connections can be made?

Author Bio:

Maria is the author of the Amazon best-selling series *The Coal Elf Chronicles*, *The Altered Experience*, and *The Aestrangel Trinity*. When not writing about dark fantasy and horror, she teaches Language Arts and Journalism to middle school students in Florida. A lover of all things dark and demented, she takes pleasure in warping the comfort factor in her readers' minds. Just when you think you've reached a safe space in her stories, she snaps you back into her twisted reality.

Discover more at
4HorsemenPublications.com

10% off using HORSEMEN10